"You're safe with me, and I'll make sure to keep you that way.

"The team secured a room for us at the Blue Ridge Lodge outside of town. We know now that you were targeted. That makes you safer with us until we find Nash, and we will find him."

She gnawed her bottom lip. "One room?"

"It'll be crowded but secure. My team and brothers will come and go as the investigation moves along. And don't worry, contrary to local legend, the Garrett men were raised to be gentlemen."

She pinned him with a fiercely ornery smile. "I was raised to be a princess. Look how that turned out. I'm about to spend the night with a man I just met."

He shot the ceiling another look and rearranged his ball cap. If the job didn't kill him, protecting Marissa Lane might.

FEDERAL AGENT UNDER FIRE

JULIE ANNE LINDSEY

Dedicated to double-shot espressos.

PLEASE RECYCLE • THIS PRODUCT IS RECYCLABLE •

Recycling programs for this product may not exist in your area.

ISBN-13: 978-1-335-52633-5

Federal Agent Under Fire

This edition published by arrangement with Harlequin Books S.A.

For questions and comments about the quality of this book, please contact us at CustomerService@Harlequin.com.

Printed in U.S.A.

Julie Anne Lindsey is a multi-genre author who writes the stories that keep her up at night. She's a self-proclaimed nerd with a penchant for words and proclivity for fun. Julie lives in rural Ohio with her husband and three small children. Today, she hopes to make someone smile. One day she plans to change the world. Julie is a member of the International Thriller Writers (ITW) and Sisters in Crime (SinC). Learn more about Julie Anne Lindsey at julieannelindsey.com.

Harlequin Intrigue

Protectors of Cade County

Federal Agent Under Fire

Visit the Author Profile page at Harlequin.com.

CAST OF CHARACTERS

Marissa Lane—Nearly abducted on her morning jog through the national forest in Shadow Point, Kentucky, this nature photographer is horrified to learn her attacker's MO matches that of a serial killer whose trail went cold five years prior.

Blake Garrett—The FBI agent is thrilled to get a new lead on the killer he came face-to-face with during his rookie year. He'd hesitated then, and the man escaped. A mistake Blake hasn't let go and one he's determined to make right. That is if he can stay focused on the case and not on the killer's latest target, a strong-willed beauty who may be Blake's undoing.

Nash Barclay—A serial killer with a wedding fetish who slipped through the fingers of a young Agent Garrett. Nash had enjoyed the ensuing chase until recently, when Blake stopped looking for him. Now Nash is back and determined to regain Agent Garrett's attention.

West Garrett—Cade County sheriff and younger brother of Blake, willing to do whatever it takes to support his brother and protect his hometown.

Kara Lane—Marissa's little sister. A nature lover who went missing on her daily hike through the mountains shortly after Marissa identified Nash Barclay as her attacker on the local news.

Cole Garrett—Youngest of four Garrett brothers and a Cade County deputy, Cole is all in to back up his brothers and capture the serial killer stalking his hometown streets.

Chapter One

Marissa Lane knew something was wrong the minute she saw him. In the six months since she'd started her predawn ritual, she'd rarely seen anyone in the national park before sunup, save the occasional ranger, but there were no rangers today. Only *him.* A man nearly engulfed in shadows at the lookout where she watched the sunrise three days a week.

She slowed her pace before reaching the low wooden fence that separated hikers from a sharp plummet into fog-laced evergreens, angling her body to keep the man in her sights. Everything about the moment set her intuition on edge, but she forced the shaky feeling away. She'd met plenty of fellow hikers over the years, and they'd all been kind. Kindred spirits. Glad to be outdoors. It was the hour that threw her. She'd started to think of herself as the only one in town who enjoyed a good sunrise.

The rocky eastern face of the park's tallest mountain was the best place in Cade County to watch a sunrise, maybe the best in Kentucky. Marissa had yet to find a better one, though it was her job to try, and she did four mornings a week. Normally, she'd have finished her water and enjoyed her apple before walking back to her ride, parked nearly five miles down the trail, but today every cell in her body said that whatever had brought this man into her path wasn't good, and she didn't want any part of it.

"Mornin'." His voice was low and gravelly. The hood of his jacket was up, working in collaboration with the shadows to shield his face.

Marissa lifted her chin in acknowledgement. She moved her tired body another step away, feigning interest in the view closest to the trail. He'd probably come there to think and was feeling as intruded upon as she was. Courtesy said she should be on her way. Greedily, she dawdled for one more breathtaking look.

The fiery glow of daylight scorched a path across the sky, climbing the opposite mountain with vigor and bathing thousands of deciduous trees, already dressed in rich autumn colors, with luminous shades from amber to apricot and everything in between. These were her favorite seconds of the day; when an ordinary forest became an inferno, and the world was backlit by Mother Nature's glory.

The man broke free from the shadow and took a few casual steps in Marissa's direction, setting her intuition into overdrive. The light scent of cigarette smoke plumed from his clothes, tainting the crisp morning air. This man wasn't a hiker, wasn't a runner, and he was definitely not getting a second of Marissa's time.

She turned away with a frustrated sigh and headed

down the mountain on tired, burning legs and a heart full of injustice. Anger churned in her gut with each forced step. She'd made the run in record time. She'd pushed her body for results and had gotten them. These few fleeting moments of sunrise were supposed to be her reward, but this man, whoever he was, was stealing those from her. She hated herself for letting him. For fearing him when she didn't know him. For denying herself the hard-earned prize because she was a woman and he was a stranger. All feminism aside, wrong or right, she'd promised her parents long ago to make safety paramount while she was on her adventures. It was her duty to hold to that, even now, when he had her sunrise and she had a long walk back to where she'd started.

The return trip was always a slower, more methodical process. A pleasurable cooldown, normally preceded by rest on the lookout. She massaged the warm muscles in her neck and shoulders as she moved, swinging her arms across her body for an added stretch. Her legs were rubbery beneath her, but the brisk autumn breeze was invigorating as it rushed over the sheen of sweat on her skin. If she could sell everything and live in the wild for a year, at one with nature, part of the beautiful multicolored kingdom around her, she'd do it in a heartbeat. But only for a year. Eventually she'd miss her crazy family, except for her little sister. Kara would probably be swinging in the hammock beside hers.

Back at the trailhead, the lot was empty except for her old Jeep, and Marissa couldn't bring herself to make the drive home without enjoying the moment of reflection she'd worked for. She checked the empty trail behind her, then hooked a left onto the short path toward Shadow Valley Lake. A hundred yards later, she slid onto the ground at the base of an ancient tree and pulled her knees to her chest. The lake was beautiful, peaceful and full of history.

Shadow Valley was one of Kentucky's lake towns. Someday Marissa planned to see for herself what remained of the underwater historic town. Records showed that residents were relocated up the mountain in the nineteen thirties before their town was permanently flooded. Hard to believe remnants of another time had stood silently beneath the surface for decades, disguised as part of the national park. Those were images she'd love to capture.

She sipped her water and wondered if she'd been irrational to change her daily routine for the sake of one man. Maybe, but what was he doing there? Where was his car, if not in the lot with hers? And who hiked five miles to have a cigarette? The scent had been strong and fresh.

She shook away the irrelevant thoughts and focused instead on the beauty before her. It was important that she start her days at peace, in harmony with her work. Marissa's adventure photos were fast becoming a lucrative business. The images she'd captured were used across the country in textbooks and at seminars on the preservation of wildlife. Her dreams were coming true and demand was rising.

In the last year alone, she'd made more than enough to pay the bills and support her travels.

She ran a forearm over her brow before crunching into her morning apple. The sweet scent lifted a smile on her lips as she pressed her tired back against the supportive tree and breathed. Her eyelids dipped closed on the exhale. The moment was so perfectly Zen; she almost didn't turn around when the sound of snapping twigs forced her eyes open. Almost.

Marissa pushed slowly to her feet, listening hard for the next noise. Whatever had cracked the twigs was heavier than a rabbit and less stealthy than anything calling this area home. She opened her stance and braced her tired form. The sudden silence was astounding. She dared a peek around the large oak. There was nothing but the breeze and a pair of chasing squirrels, turning century-old trees into a playground. She puffed a sigh of relief.

The breeze lifted again, stronger this time and bringing a fresh rustling of leaves with it. This distinct scent of cigarette smoke stiffened her spine. Logically, she knew she wasn't in danger. She'd visited the national park three days a week and met dozens of people, all friendly. But her logic had already shut down. Marissa discarded her apple. She screwed the lid on her bottle and gripped it in both hands.

A jaunty whistle lifted slowly into the air and echoed off the trees. A strange, familiar tune she hadn't heard in years, and one that seemed wildly out of place in the forest.

She stepped silently around the tree and again, there was nothing.

Except the whistle.

Marissa turned in a small circle, seeking the source. Her accelerated heartbeat joined every other instinct telling her to go. She bounced forward, away from the sound, back toward the trail. To the safety of her Jeep. The normalcy of her life.

"Don't leave." A man's voice boomed in her ear, successfully ending the whistle and shattering the eerie silence left in its wake.

Something hard connected with the side of her head, sending her sideways into another large tree. Scents of earth and bark exploded in her senses as sharp pain tore through her face. Marissa cried out at the shock and agony. The sound was extinguished by a large pair of gloved hands, clamping firmly around her throat.

Softly then, the man began to sing.

Her eyes bulged. Searing pressure filled her lungs. She clawed uselessly at the massive hands until images of her sister and parents blurred in her mind. She was dying, and he was singing.

Suddenly her fight-or-flight instinct sharpened like a switchblade slicing through the fear. No longer able to flee, years of self-defense courses bubbled to the cloudy surface of her thoughts along with the voices of past instructors, her father, and every surviving woman whose story had served as a warning.

Marissa refused to be a victim.

She released his hands and balled her fingers into

fists. She rammed her elbows into the soft torso behind her and drew strength from the gust of breath that swept out of him in response. She stomped one foot against her attacker's instep and followed with a kick to the shin. He swore violently and tightened the pressure on her throat, repositioning his fingers for a more effective grip. Black dots danced in her peripheral vision, but she wasn't done. *The human kneecap breaks with only eight pounds of pressure.* He was taller than her, but slower. She kicked again, raising her foot high behind her, this time earning a wild yelp. His grip faltered and sweet oxygen rushed into her burning lungs. She was small, but that was an advantage, not a curse. She bent her knees to lower her center of gravity and clutched his forearms with both hands. In one final heave, her body lurched forward, chucking the man over her back and soundly onto his. Air whooshed from his mouth, and Marissa's wobbly legs were in motion before he'd hit the ground.

FEDERAL AGENT BLAKE GARRETT stormed into the Shadow Point Sheriff's Department with a familiar mix of dread and adrenaline. "West." His voice echoed through the building as his long legs ate up the distance between the front desk and his brother West's office. He dipped his chin at the receptionist as he passed. If West was right about Nash Barclay, there was no time to waste on formalities.

"West." Blake strode past a set of deputies gearing up for their shift and down the narrow hall past

West's empty office. The place never changed. Concrete floors. Metal desks. The constant aroma of black coffee in the air, and the words *Sheriff Garrett* painted on the big office door. The Garrett inside was once their father. Now, it was his younger brother. *Where the hell was he?*

Blake opened his mouth to call again, but stopped short.

Sheriff West Garrett popped his head through the open conference room door. "Hey." He met Blake with a hearty hug. "It's good to see you. Wish I could get you back to town this quick for fishing and birthdays, but I suppose a possible serial killer sighting is as good an invitation for you." West's hair was lighter than Blake's, bleached by hours in the sun. His face was tanned and his eyes were bright, mischievous for a reason Blake couldn't comprehend. They had business to discuss. Ugly, dirty business and no reason, as far as Blake could tell, for nonsense.

"How sure are you that this was Nash?" Blake asked. He owed Nash Barclay a bullet and he planned on making good on the debt. "He's been underground for nearly five years."

West furrowed his brows. "When was the last time you slept, man?"

Roughly? Five years ago. "I'm doing just fine, Mom. Now, can we get down to business, or do you want to ask me if I'm getting enough to eat?" Blake forced a smile to smooth the sharp edge of his words. Yes, he'd been away more than around these last few years, but he'd had good reason. He didn't feel right showing his face in a town where he'd let a serial killer get away. Who would?

"All right." West nodded. "Cole and I agree the victim fits the profile. Blond hair, blue eyes, petite build." He circled a wrist, implying Blake knew the rest.

Four women had gone missing during Blake's rookie year at the bureau, and he'd worked long and hard to find a connection between them when no one else could. Beyond their appearances the women had nothing in common. On the surface. Once Blake had started pulling threads, he found the same toxic creature hidden in all their lives—Nash Barclay. Nash had worked as a maintenance man for the local library system, and each of his victims had frequented a branch where Nash made regular service calls. Blake went to pick him up for questioning, but Nash ran. He'd tried to lose Blake in the labyrinth of industrial park alleys and abandoned factories but Shadow Point was Blake's home turf, and Nash was soon confronted with the business end of Blake's department issued Glock. They'd stood ten feet apart on a sprawling asphalt roof at the old tire plant, daring one another to make a move. Nash had taunted him, screaming obscenities until he was red-faced, begged him to shoot or go home, but Blake had been determined to stick to protocols, obey procedures, wait for his partner. He wanted Nash in cuffs, not in the morgue. He'd relived the moment a thousand times, certain he'd done everything right *until Nash began to sing.*

Nash's mood had changed in an instant. The violence in his expression had morphed into an eerie smile, and he'd sang. The behavior had successfully fractured Blake's concentration, and in that splinter of a second, while Blake had pondered the mind of a psychopath, Nash dove headlong over the roof's edge. He'd landed on the shorter building next door with ease and disappeared behind a massive smokestack. For the last five years, he might as well have been the smoke.

The moment should have ended in an arrest. A victory for justice. It should have catapulted Blake's budding career. Instead, it had put him on a short list of screw-ups. Worse, his mistake had cost those missing women and their families the justice they deserved. That moment had changed his life and caused him to question everything, especially himself.

"And the song?" Blake asked. "She said he sang the song?"

"Yep." West leaned closer. "Why don't we go over things in my office?"

"First, I need coffee." Blake stepped forward.

West's arm bobbed up like a guard gate, blocking the conference room doorway. "We should talk first."

Blake stopped to look more closely at his brother. West never said no to coffee. "Why?"

"Well, I guess because Miss Lane's eager to meet you." He twisted his mouth into a knot.

"Great."

West grinned. "She'd like another crack at the man who attacked her. Thinks you can use her help."

Blake snorted. "I need a lot of things right now, but help from a little blonde woman isn't one of them. I need coffee and whatever information you gained from her interview, then I'll stop by the victim's place after you've debriefed me. See if she's thought of anything else that can help us."

West shook his head. "I'm trying to tell you she didn't go home."

"Parents' house?"

"Nope."

"Well, where'd she go?" Blake cocked a hip, resting a restless hand over the butt of his sidearm. "Boyfriend's place?" That'd be a first. Nash had specifically chosen single women in the past.

West dropped his arm and tilted his head toward the conference room. "She's waiting for you."

"What?" He craned his head for a better look through the doorway. "Why didn't you send her home?" He dropped his voice to a whisper and checked his watch. "Do you mean to tell me she's been sitting in there for more than two hours? You should've driven her home by now." He pushed West's arm out of his way and strode into the conference room. Blake stopped short at the sight of a clearly aggravated woman in running gear.

"I'm not a victim," she said. "Also, the sheriff tried to send me home, but I'm not one to be sent anywhere, especially when I can be useful. Someone's trolling the park for women, and I can help." Her disheveled ponytail was hanging on by threads, but her backbone was straight as an arrow.

Blake's cheek twitched. He cast an uneasy glance at his brother. "This is Miss Lane?"

West smiled. "I tried to get you to go with me to my office."

The woman was on her feet and moving in Blake's direction. "I'm Marissa Lane." She shoved a little hand his way. "It's nice to meet you, Agent Garrett. I wish it was under different circumstances."

Blake agreed. Marissa had managed to shock and impress him in under a minute. A task no one had ever accomplished, and Blake had met a lot of people.

"Miss Lane," he began in his most calming tone. "Thank you for your willingness to help. You've undergone an incredible trauma today, but I'd like to ask you a few more questions. Let me know if you need to stop at any point during the interview. We can take a break or pick up tomorrow. Whatever you'd like. I assume you've already told the sheriff everything you can recall."

"I have." She nodded. "If I understand correctly, you believe the man who attacked me is responsible for taking several women."

"It's a distinct possibility, yes. That's what I'm here to find out."

"Well, I have no intention of going home until I've told you everything I told your brother and accompanied you back to the park. I'd like to show you where it happened." She shot a pointed look at Blake's black dress shoes. "I hope you brought a change of clothes."

Blake dragged his gaze to the space behind him where West was retreating toward his office.

Blake unbuttoned his suit jacket and took a seat at the large oval table in the room's center, attempting to regain control of the situation. He cleared his throat and turned his face to the spitfire before him. She certainly looked like Nash's type. Obviously beautiful. Small features. Narrow frame. The clingy blue jogging pants and matching tank top left little to the imagination in terms of her shape. Blake's hands could easily cover the span of her waist. A very Southern-debutante appeal, but looks were deceiving. He fought a smile as he imagined the shock Nash must've had when this little woman kicked his ass.

"Agent?" Her voice drew him back like a slap in the face.

"Sorry." Blake shifted on his seat and gauged his words carefully. He also did his best to clear a few unprofessional thoughts from his mind. "The man I'm after is six feet tall, and he's probably got seventy-five pounds on you." Give or take the few that five years might have delivered.

Marissa crossed her arms. "And?"

Blake's cheek twitched again. Twice in ten minutes. She was funny. Did she know she was funny? "How'd you do it?"

"I fought." Marissa lifted a tuft of fallen hair off her cheek and hooked it over one ear, revealing a thick crimson line along her jawbone and faint purple bruising under the corresponding eye. "He grabbed me. Hit me. Choked me. I used my size against him. Would you like a demonstration?"

Somewhere in the next room, West coughed.

Blake gave the shared wall a dirty look before turning his attention back to Marissa Lane. "That won't be necessary." He opened a notebook and clicked his pen to life. "Has anyone evaluated your injuries?"

Marissa nodded. "Cole," she said.

"Good."

Cole was the youngest Garrett brother, a former army medic and a certified EMT. He was also a medical school dropout, but he hated when the family brought that up.

"West insisted I choose between Cole or a trip to the ER," Marissa added. "I figured, at least I know Cole."

Blake nodded, hoping the fact she had no bandages meant the injuries appeared worse than they actually were.

"Why don't you have a seat and start by telling me what you remember?"

She turned to pace the room. "I remember being grabbed from behind, hit across the face and nearly dragged into the forest. The assailant was your brother's height, West's, not Cole's." She waved a dismissive hand. "I went to high school with them. Never dreamed they'd become the town sheriff and deputy, but I guess I should have. Whatever happened to Ryder?"

"He's a US Marshal."

She cocked an eyebrow, as if to say more on the topic, but shook her head and stayed on task. "The lunatic was singing that old song. 'Going to the Chapel'."

Blake tapped his pen against the notepad. He'd have to ask how well she knew his brothers later. He'd left for college before they'd started high school. A curious sense of frustration knotted inside him.

Marissa dropped her arms to her sides. "Did you always want to work for the FBI?"

"No." The Garretts were a family of law enforcement and everyone in Cade County knew it, but Blake never wanted to be sheriff. Though there was a certain pressure for Blake to conform, he'd wanted to do something bigger than hand out traffic tickets and break up marital disputes. He'd gone as far as to finish his law degree, dreaming of a judgeship, before the allure of a shiny badge had caught up with him. Something about those coveted initials, FBI, had changed his life plan without warning.

Marissa leaned her slender backside against the table and crossed her ankles. Soft, distracting scents of coconut and pineapple lifted off her. "Whoever he was, I caught him off guard. I left him on his back by the lake and ran until I saw a car. I flagged the guy down and asked him to drop me off here. My car's still at the base camp parking lot. I had to run in the opposite direction, and I was afraid to double back. I can pick it up when we go see the crime scene."

THE SWOON-WORTHY AGENT stretched onto his feet and loomed over Marissa. His sharp blue eyes cut a line across her bruised face, lingering at her equally sore collarbone before returning to her eyes. "Fine. We can talk more on the way."

He patted a rhythm on the wall, and his brothers appeared. "Give me five minutes to change, then follow us up to the lake."

The men exchanged looks and broke off in three separate directions.

Several minutes later, Blake returned in a pair of low-slung jeans, military boots and a slate-gray T-shirt. He'd screwed a plain navy ball cap over his thick dark hair and covered his serious blue eyes with tinted aviators. An impressive FBI badge completed the look. "Time to saddle up."

Marissa followed a line of Garrett men to their cars. She smoothed her hair and straightened her shirt, uncertain if the bubbling of nerves in her core was caused by a return to the crime scene or something else entirely. Plenty of women's daydreams had begun like this in Shadow Point. Alone with multiple uniformed Garretts. Fortunately, Marissa had spent four years of high school learning about the inevitable heartbreak a lady could expect from any one of those unbelievably attractive packages. What she couldn't figure out was why Blake Garrett had thrown her off balance? The others didn't faze her, but they also didn't command a room with their presence the way Blake did. If she remembered correctly, he was just four years older than West. Five years older than her. He'd left town long before she'd thought about guys beyond their inability to beat her at anything at all.

The men stopped beside a big black pickup. The truck hadn't been in the lot when Marissa arrived. Blake pointed a fob in the truck's direction and the locks popped up. "Miss Lane?" He extended his hand. "Boost?"

Why not? She grabbed the open door frame in one hand and placed her opposite palm on Blake's. His warm, calloused skin sent a jolt of electricity through her. Blake closed strong fingers over hers and waited as she bounced into the cab.

The door snapped shut behind her, and the Garretts circled up, speaking too low for her to understand. The men seemed to take turns examining her through the closed window. Blake adjusted his ball cap a few times before breaking free from the group and swinging into the driver's seat.

"Everything okay?" she asked.

"No." He slid his eyes in her direction briefly, checked the rearview, and gunned the engine to life. "Someone attacked you today. That's a big problem, and I plan to fix it."

Chapter Two

Blake slowed his truck at the national park entrance where a line of cars blocked the gate. A park ranger moved car to car, waving his hands and pointing toward the exit.

"What the hell?" Blake powered his window down and shoved an elbow over the frame. He tipped his head through the open window. "Hey, what's going on?"

The ranger, still two cars away, shot him a dirty look and continued arguing with the driver of a rusted hatchback.

Blake shifted into Park and climbed down from the cab. He gave Marissa an authoritative stare. "Stay put."

She released her seat belt and twisted on the seat, scanning the scene outside. A big white van with a satellite on top came into view, along with a cluster of people and cameras. "This day keeps getting worse."

"What?" Blake peered over the crush of stalled vehicles. "The reporter?"

"I think the good Samaritan who drove me to the sheriff's department is being interviewed by that news crew."

"Sonofa—" Blake slammed his door and headed into the chaos. His FBI shield bounced against his chest on a beaded metal chain. "Hey," he called again, "what's this about?"

The ranger sagged in relief. He motioned to Blake's badge. "Sorry. I didn't know you were FBI. It's pandemonium up here."

"You want to fill me in?" Blake asked.

"Some guy showed up with a news crew an hour ago. He says a woman was attacked here this morning. They aired a live interview snippet, and people started pouring in to have a look at the crime scene. Campers are scared. Some are leaving. The phone won't stop ringing."

Blake could barely hear the phone inside the little guard booth. He climbed onto a massive tree stump painted with the park hours and strained for a better look at the crowd near the white van. A man in Dickies and flannel stood beside a woman Blake recognized from the Channel Six News team. If that man hadn't saved Marissa, Blake would've been tempted to escort him out of the park violently.

The ranger fixed Blake with an expectant look. "What should we do?"

As if on cue, the sheriff's cruiser rolled into view, bouncing through the grass alongside a line of waiting cars. Blake whistled and waved to his brothers as

West angled between the guard gate and overcrowded lot. No other cars would get in until he moved.

Cole jumped out. “We’ve got this. You got her?” He flicked his gaze to Blake’s truck.

Blake nodded and shook the ranger’s hand, eager to get back to Marissa. “Sheriff and Deputy Garrett will take it from here.” He jogged back to the truck and climbed inside. “You okay?”

“Fine.”

“Good.” He wrenched his truck free from the line and parked it in the grass beside the news van.

He pocketed the keys and turned for Marissa. “Ready?” The alarm in her eyes stunned him into silence. She’d put on a brave face at the station, but there was no confidence in her expression now. A distant part of him longed to comfort her somehow, but that wasn’t his place. She probably had a long line of people waiting to fold her into their arms and ease her fear. Blake’s job was to stop a madman.

She turned weary eyes on him. “Yes.”

“Don’t worry.” The statement was out before he’d thought better of it. Then, already heading downhill, he made it worse. “I won’t let him hurt you again.” The words soured on his tongue. How could he promise to protect her? He’d let Nash get away once already. Wasn’t it technically his fault that Nash had gotten ahold of her at all?

Marissa lifted her chin and rolled her shoulders back. “Thank you for saying so, but I’m not afraid.” The lie was evident in the lines gathered across her forehead, but Blake didn’t argue.

He climbed out and met Marissa on her side of the truck. "Why don't you take me to where you left him?"

"Sure." Marissa led the way down a gravel and mud path from Blake's makeshift parking spot to the trailhead. "I started here around five thirty."

"Miss?" A woman's voice carried over the drone of the crowd. "Miss? Excuse me." The Channel Six reporter hurried in Marissa's direction waving a microphone. Her pink dress suit and pearls were sorely out of place in the park. Her pointy heels sank into the ground with each hurried step. Worse, she wasn't alone. She was a mama duck, trailed by her cameraman, the guy who'd driven Marissa to the station and a row of nosy locals craning to get a look at the victim.

Marissa made a soft squeaky noise and Blake's hackles rose. He widened his stance and lifted a palm in the reporter's direction. "Stop right there."

"Absolutely." She fluffed her hair and straightened her jacket. "I'm Linda Somers, Channel Six News. And you are?" She eyeballed the badge around his neck. A sugary-sweet smile curved her lips.

The cameraman positioned himself near a tree and hoisted the camera onto one shoulder, arranging his shot. A little red light blinked at the side of his lens. He gave Linda a thumbs-up.

Her smile widened. "Are you here to investigate this morning's attack, Federal Agent…" She left the sentence hanging.

"That's Blake Garrett," someone called from the crowd. "He's the sheriff's brother."

Damn small towns. Blake ground his teeth. "Please direct your questions to Sheriff Garrett."

"Is this the victim?" she asked. Pencil-thin eyebrows rose behind her bangs.

The man who'd called this fiasco into action nodded. "Yeah. That's her. I found her running along the county road, crying."

"You're certain?" the reporter asked.

"Positive. I wouldn't forget picking up a lady dressed like that."

Marissa wrapped both arms around her middle and glared at the man. Her outfit might not be camera ready, but she was dressed appropriately for a run, which was likely the only thing she'd expected to do before her shower.

Blake groaned. "She has no comment." He moved between Marissa and the reporter.

The cameraman honed in on them.

"What's your name, Miss?" Linda asked. "Are you from Cade County? Do you come here often? How long have you known Federal Agent Garrett?"

Heat from Marissa's body warmed his side. Her fingers pressed against his back as she stepped into view of the mob forming along the trailhead. He should've guessed she'd refuse to stay behind him. Fire churned in his gut. The bigmouthed reporter had taken the only tactical advantage Blake had over Nash—surprise. Now, Nash would know Blake was there, and the games would begin again before Blake was ready.

Blake scanned the crowd for his enemy. What if seeing him with Marissa fueled Nash's need to get his hands on her again? What if Blake's presence put her in more danger? As if the fact she'd gotten away wasn't reason enough for him to come at her again.

West and Cole arrived a moment later, waving their badges and hollering instructions at the crowd.

"That's our cue." Blake wound his fingers around Marissa's wrist and tugged. "Let them take care of the crowd. Let's get back to what we came for."

MARISSA TOOK THE LEAD, but her stomach protested the trip, and her limbs strained against her. Instinct begged her never to return to the place where she'd nearly been abducted, but resolve pushed her forward. Whether she wanted to go or not was irrelevant. Who knew how many more women would be in danger if the man who grabbed her wasn't caught? Images of the awful moments flooded her mind, lifting the fine hairs along the back of her neck, and resurrecting another memory. A shiver rolled through her.

"What's wrong?" Blake's voice was low and cautious.

She scrubbed a hand over her lips. "I'm not sure. Maybe nothing."

"Let's hear it."

"There was a man who tossed bread crumbs into the lake this summer. He was always there when I came back from my morning runs. That guy had a black hoodie like the man I saw today at the lookout. I know it's not much, and everyone owns a black hoodie, but it could be something, right?"

"Anything could be something. You saw him more than once?"

She squinted against the brilliant sunlight, desperate for a more useful memory or detail. "He was there every morning for a while. Then, one day he just wasn't."

"Did he see you?"

"I think so. I'm hard to miss after five miles up and down a mountain." She heaved a sigh. "I probably looked a lot like this, except swinging my arms to cool down from the jog." Marissa plucked stringy bangs off her forehead and groaned inwardly. For the first time since she'd arrived at the station, she was fiercely self-conscious. Why hadn't she at least combed her hair or washed her face while she'd waited on Blake to arrive? It was bad enough she was bruised and dirty. She didn't have to be a disheveled nightmare, too. "I'm a mess."

"You've gone over ten miles on foot today and fought off a man twice your size. I think you get a pass."

So, he agreed. She was a mess. She pulled her ponytail down and shook her hair out, raking fingers through the tangles. She stopped moving when the lake came into view.

Shadow Valley Lake was nearly eighteen square miles of water, much of it surrounded by tall grasses, angry geese and a well-beaten path courtesy of Cade County fishermen. Her apple, now covered in ants, lay in the grass near a massive oak tree. "I was there. Eating that apple." She regretted leaving the trash behind. "I'll take that with me when I leave this time."

Blake examined the ground near her apple. "The apple's evidence now. Look." He pushed the grass back and forth with his shoe, revealing two sets of imprints. Her Nikes and a pair of boots. He hovered his foot near the larger print. He fished his cell phone from one pocket and took pictures of the discovery.

Emotion coiled in Marissa's gut. Her eyes stung, and her bottom lip trembled. She sipped cool air and forced her mind away from the vivid memories clawing at her heart. "The man with the bread crumbs was always right there." She pointed to a crescent of mud and rock at the massive lake's edge.

They moved toward the spot. Boot imprints striped the soft earth, as if he'd been pacing. "Do you see those?" she asked.

"Yep." He snapped another picture. "Same tread pattern as the prints by your apple."

Marissa bit into her thumbnail. No one had been at the lake on her predawn trip up the mountain, and she hadn't seen anyone when she sat under the tree to enjoy her apple.

Blake scanned the area with sharp, trained eyes. He mumbled something under his breath and raised his phone again, this time for a picture of the lake.

Marissa followed his icy stare to a sprinkling of white flecks on the glassy surface. "Is that bread?"

"No." Blake turned his phone over and tapped the screen. "Those are white rose petals."

Marissa wrinkled her nose. "There aren't any white roses in the park."

"Hey," Blake growled into the phone, now pressed to his ear. "Get me a cast kit. We've got pattern evidence at the lake." He disconnected and gripped the cell phone in his palm. "Any chance the man you saw here a few months ago could've been tossing these onto the water instead of bread crumbs?"

"Maybe. Why? What do they mean?" She tried to hide the fear settling in her bones.

Blake rubbed the back of his neck. "The fugitive I've been chasing left white rose petals on the doorstep of his victims' homes."

"I'm guessing you don't think these petals are a coincidence." Marissa's stomach sank as she watched the little white boats skating across the serene water.

Blake snapped more pictures of the petals. "I don't believe in coincidence."

Well, they had that in common. She turned away and closed her eyes, engaging painful memories. "He was singing 'Going to the Chapel' and leaves roses. Does he have a fantasy about marrying his victims?"

"I don't know. He wasn't very forthcoming when I tried to haul him in, and we never found the women, but I assume this is all part of some sick fetish. He lost a girlfriend to suicide about a year before he took his first victim."

Marissa opened her eyes and headed back to her fallen apple. She worked methodically around the grass, parting the blades with her shoe like Blake had. Maybe she could find a clue, too. Something Blake could send to the crime lab where his science and tech people worked.

Something moved in the distance. A few seconds later, Cole appeared with a backpack.

"How well do you know Cole?" Blake asked. He stopped a few feet ahead of her and waved to his brother. "You went to school together. Anything else?"

"Not really." She tented her brows. Was she being accused of something? "We live in a small town and went to the same high school. We ran into each other from time to time. West and Ryder, too."

Blake turned at the waist and narrowed his eyes on her. She knew all three of his little brothers, but he hadn't met her until today? A nagging sense of injustice registered at the back of his mind.

"What?" She bounced her toe against something hard, and a little navy pouch flipped into view. "Hey, look at this." Marissa crouched over the object. Recognition swept through her like a hurricane, sucking air from her lungs and pushing her attention in a new direction. She stood on wooden legs and stared at the tranquil lake behind them.

"What is that?" Blake crouched where she had been a moment before.

Marissa pressed a palm to her roiling stomach. She owned several pouches just like that one. "It's a one-pound weight. They're used on scuba belts."

Cole settled in beside Blake and handed him the backpack.

Marissa pushed windblown hair from her eyes while the men bagged their evidence. Blades of ice seemed to wedge in her chest. “I know where he might’ve hidden those women’s bodies. I’d planned to do a photo shoot there soon.”

“Where?” the Garretts asked in near unison.

She lifted a finger toward the lake. *The rose petals. The creepy song.* “I think they’re in Shadow Valley.” Cade County’s historic lake town, submerged long ago in the name of flood control.

BLAKE MADE THE necessary calls to rouse a dive crew and the remainder of his team from Louisville. The agents arrived in just over an hour. The divers were another story, being parceled together from approved volunteers across the state, policemen, game wardens, anyone trained and available to thoroughly explore the remnants of an entire underwater town, door by door if necessary, while preserving as much potential evidence as possible. He’d also called in a favor with a local private security firm for additional help clearing the park and tending the curious crowd, which had been pushed outside the gates.

The space around the normally tranquil lake bustled with speculation and activity. Once all the divers arrived, things would get worse, and if Marissa’s hunch was right, more gruesome.

Her hunch. Not his.

Blake mentally kicked himself for never considering Shadow Valley Lake as a place to hide four bodies. If memory served, the Shadow Valley Chapel was one of the buildings swallowed by the lake. Finding victims in the underwater chapel would raise the stakes impossibly higher. That kind of discovery would suggest Nash was smarter and more resourceful than Blake had given him credit for. He'd always assumed Nash was the impulsive type, more likely to hide his crimes in a hurry than with careful planning and scuba gear. In fact, he'd considered Nash lucky for getting away at all. He'd blamed his own rookie hesitation.

Blake pressed the heels of his hands against closed eyes. What if Blake had been wrong all these years? What if the real mistake he'd made was underestimating Nash? The possibility came with all sorts of ugly thoughts. Blake had linked him to four missing women, but what if there were more? How many cases hadn't he connected? What had Nash been doing these last five years while Blake chased his tail? Blake had assumed Nash was hiding, but what if Nash was still killing and Blake had missed it?

He scrubbed open palms over his face and forehead. *How long had Nash been planning to take Marissa?*

His attention cut through the collection of lawmen to where she rested her head against an oak tree not far from the lake. Her swollen eyes were shut. Her cheeks were red. The bruises from her attack had grown more pronounced as the day wore on, making Blake angrier with each passing second.

He couldn't seem to find it in himself to be thankful she was safe. He could only grow more infuriated that she'd been hurt.

She opened her eyes as he approached, a look of shock and panic on her face.

He lifted a hand and crouched beside her. "It's only me. How are you holding up?"

"Fine." Her knees bobbed with misplaced adrenaline. "Anything new?"

"The rest of the divers should be here soon, but it's a big lake. It's going to take them some time to search an entire town."

She sat forward, hugging bent knees to her chest. "I have street maps for the town under the lake at my place. I could go get them. I'd hoped to take photos for a magazine interested in doing a spread on lake towns. The maps could save the divers time."

Blake rested his forearms across his thighs, dangling both hands between his knees. "We have the town blueprint. Right now, the divers are fighting daylight to get here, and they haven't got much left." He stretched onto his feet and extended a hand to hoist her up. "How do you feel about taking a walk while we wait?"

She accepted his hand. "Where are we going?"

"You said you saw a man at the lookout. We should get up there while the park's closed to visitors." He motioned for her to lead the way.

Marissa stopped at the base of Sunrise Trail. She cocked a hip and stared up the dirt path. Uncertainty flashed in her eyes. "I didn't get a good look at the guy up there, but he smelled like cigarette smoke." She braced a hand to her forehead like a visor and squinted against the sun. "The man who attacked me also smelled like smoke, but I suppose that's hardly enough to conclude it was the same man."

"Do you think it was the same man?"

She cast her gaze to the ground. "I do."

Blake motioned her forward. "That's good enough for me."

She took a deep breath and began her second five-mile uphill hike of the day. At least this time she wasn't running. "I was a little spooked to see someone at the lookout before dawn. Confused, too. My car was the only one in the lot."

Blake turned an amused expression on her. "You hiked five miles before dawn." He shook his head in apparent awe. "You're making me regret the coffee and cruller breakfast I had on my way here from Louisville."

Marissa smiled. "Well, if it helps, I didn't hike. I ran."

He laughed. "Oh, yeah. That makes me feel much better. Thank you."

She fell into a comfortable stride and inhaled deeply, finding as much inner peace as possible on this horrific day. "I run every morning, but three days a week I do it here. I like the view, and I normally enjoy the solitude." She bit her lip against the tirade that had been swirling in her mind for the past few hours. "I knew something was wrong. I knew it, and I didn't leave."

Blake stopped moving and stared at her. "You couldn't have known. Even if you had, you weren't at fault here. Don't let that worm get into your head. From what I can tell, you did everything right, and if this man is who I think he is, you're the first to get away. You should be proud of yourself."

"Really? Because it was pride that kept me here when my instincts told me to go home. It was pride that took me to the lake for my reward."

"Reward?"

She groaned. "It's stupid, but I beat my best time getting to the lookout, and I'd planned to reward myself by watching the sunrise. I was mad that I'd let his presence keep me from enjoying the view." She dropped her head back and laughed. "So instead of getting in my car, I made a side trip to the lake. I was that close to leaving unharmed."

Blake's face darkened. "This wasn't your fault. I don't care if he shook your hand and said, 'I'm going to attack you unless you go home.' He's still the criminal. He's the one in the wrong. Not you."

Marissa stepped over a fallen branch. "Thanks, but it's hard not to think about what I could've done differently."

Patchy sunlight filtered through the lush forest canopy. A soft breeze kicked up, lifting scents of shampoo and sweat from Blake's body.

Marissa shook her thoughts back to the situation at hand. "Can you tell me more about Nash? That's his name, right?" Her hand moved instinctually to her throat. She blinked through the fresh sting of tears. "I've heard you and your brothers use it, but no one's filled me in on the specifics."

"I linked Nash to the disappearances of four women about five years ago. The missing women were never recovered, but I know he took them. I saw it in his eyes when I confronted him." His square jawline popped and clenched. Whatever he wasn't sharing was painful and Marissa's heart hurt for him, too.

"What does he look like?" Marissa asked.

Blake cast her a sidelong glance. "I'll show you a picture when we get back. I would've done that at the station but West said you didn't see the man who attacked you."

"I didn't. I thought a description might jar my memory about the man at the lake last summer."

Blake glanced over his shoulder. "Nash has brown hair and eyes. He's six foot. Average weight, but no definition. He wasn't much to look at. No distinguishing marks, scars or tattoos. Of course, that was a while back. A lot could have happened since then."

"Was he a smoker?"

"Yes."

Ice curled through Marissa's body. She'd been in the grips of a serial killer. The bruises on her face and throat throbbed at the thought. She pressed cool fingers against the aching pains.

"I'm going to find him." Blake's voice cracked the last ounce of composure Marissa had.

A hot, fat tear broke over her cheek and slid onto her jaw. Then another.

"Hey." Blake stopped climbing. "Miss Lane." He caught her trembling hand in his as she took another step without him. He squeezed gently before releasing her.

She swiped shaky fingertips across both eyelids before daring to look back. "I'm fine. Please call me Marissa."

"You're not fine, Marissa, but you're going to be. I'm going to find this guy. I won't let him get away again." He lifted a white handkerchief in her direction.

The sincerity in Blake's voice warmed her, and the sound of her name on his lips settled her fraying nerves. "I know." She accepted the handkerchief and pressed it to her eyes, thankful for his comforting presence. "Who carries a handkerchief?"

"Me. All of us." He fumbled for words, clearly uncomfortable telling her something so personal. "My brothers and I."

Apparently, even that legendary Garrett confidence wasn't bulletproof. Marissa smiled behind the soft cotton material, enjoying the aromatic blend of Blake's soap and cologne caught in the wispy fabric. "I see." She returned his quizzical glance. "Why?"

"You ask a lot of questions."

"It's a long hike."

Blake turned his face to her and smiled. Not another lazy effort like he'd offered her before, but a true smile that reached his eyes and scaled the years away.

She'd found Blake devastatingly handsome as a straight-faced agent, but the smiling man beneath the badge was so much more. His ability to show such charm and compassion on a day as cursed as this was enough to weaken her knees. "I'd love to know, and honestly, I could use the distraction."

He paused to look her in the eye. "Our granddad gave those to us when we were small. None of us used them until his funeral a few years back, but we all carried them to the service. That was the day I started bringing mine everywhere." He looked away, into the forest, seemingly lost in the memory.

"You carry a piece of him," she mused. "That's sweet."

He extended his hand. "Give me my hanky."

She set the cloth in his hand with a smile. "You aren't what you seem, Federal Agent Garrett."

"Folks rarely are."

Chapter Three

There was nothing to see at the lookout. No clues. No boot prints. It was a five-mile walk for bust. Frustration churned in Blake's chest as he mentally replayed the morning's events. Every clue pointed directly to his nemesis, a maniac he'd dedicated years to finding. *Where are you, Nash?* Blake's muscles tensed as another terrible thought came to mind. "We need to go."

"What? Why?" Marissa followed him back down the trail at a clip. "What's happening? Did you find something?"

Blake slowed his pace by a fraction, adjusting for her shorter gait. "When was the last time you were home?"

"This morning. I left around five."

He furrowed his brow. "The rose petals."

"You want to see if he left them on my doorstep." She bobbed her head in understanding. "Well, that's completely terrifying."

Blake slowed further. "You should probably pack

a bag while we're there and make plans to stay with family for a few nights."

"Do you really think he'd come for me again? He has to know you're on to him. It was broadcast on the news."

"He'll come."

"But you were standing right beside me on the air."

"Exactly."

Marissa marched silently for several paces. "Fine, but I'm not dragging my family into this. I'll stay somewhere else."

Blake's eyes widened. "Haven't you told them what's happening?"

"Of course." She'd called her parents the minute she'd arrived at the sheriff's department and again while Blake had organized his team. "I told them everything I knew this morning, which was that a lunatic nearly abducted me in the park. Then, I filled them in on the possibility of a fugitive at large and warned my sister to stay out of the park. Dad caught the news, so he knows I'm with you. My sister's been checking in by text every hour or so to make sure I'm still out here. Still safe."

Blake scowled. "So, stay with them."

"And paint a big red X on their door? No thank you. I'm not leading a psychopath straight to my family."

"Well, you can't stay at your place."

"Fine, but I won't stay with my parents or sister either. That'll have to be good enough." Five quiet miles later, she hooked a left at the trail's base and headed for the parking lot.

Blake fired up his truck and followed her older model mud-soaked Jeep down the county road through town at just over the speed limit until houses faded into farms and farms gave way to forest. She slowed at a partially hidden drive and turned onto a narrow gravel road. His truck bounced and rocked along behind her for several minutes before a small clearing came into view.

A log cabin was situated among the trees with a portion of somewhat flat land serving as her front and back yards. Flower baskets and wind chimes hung from the porch roof and a pair of rocking chairs stood sentinel beside the door.

He met her on the porch, gun drawn. No rose petals, but the front window was open, leaving her sheer white curtains to flutter.

"Do you normally leave this open?"

"No." Marissa's fearful gaze was latched to the parted window frame. "I always check the windows before bed, and I didn't open any this morning."

Blake ran cautious fingertips around the wooden trim, stopping at the first patch of splintering, a discreet but telltale sign of tampering. He sent a text to West. They needed a deputy for fingerprints. Normally, he'd suggest the deputy talk to Marissa's neighbors, but she didn't have any.

Marissa lifted her house key on trembling fingers, and he slid it into the still locked door. With any luck, Nash was hunkered down inside, feeling overly confident and about to be reunited with his maker.

He raised a flat palm between them. "Wait here."

Marissa followed him inside and pulled the door shut.

He gave her a warning look. "I told you to wait outside."

Her pale skin and flushed cheeks said what she wouldn't. Marissa was scared.

Blake's need for vengeance warred momentarily with his desire to erase the terrified expression from her face. "Stay close."

She crossed the floor on silent feet, thanking him with wide blue eyes. Her small pink lips were pressed tight. He cleared the front room and kitchen, then crept into the narrow hallway separating her living space from the rest of the home. So far, every window in the house was open.

"What was that?" Marissa pressed her fingers against his waist.

Blake froze as something moved in the next room. He set his hand on the doorknob and motioned Marissa to step back. Slowly, she uncurled her fingers from the fabric of his shirt and inched away. With the flick of Blake's wrist, the door flung open, and he rushed inside. "Clear." Blake was alone in a brightly colored utility room, surrounded by murals of birds in trees and yellow rays of sunshine.

Marissa poked her head into the room. "Nothing?"

The curtain ruffled, and she jumped. White eyelet lace rubbed the curled pages of a worn paperback on the sill.

Blake pushed the fabric aside for a look into the backyard. "How many more rooms?"

"Three. A bathroom next door and two bedrooms across the hall."

They moved in tandem through the next two rooms, both small, cheerfully decorated and void of Nash. The last door was several paces beyond the others and closed. Marissa gasped. "I didn't close that door."

Blake squared his shoulders, and Marissa fell back again. He shoved the final door open, and a slew of swear words lodged on his tongue.

Marissa padded into the room a moment later. "Oh, no."

A wedding veil was strewn across Marissa's bed and surrounded by hundreds of white rose petals. The soft scent raised bile in Blake's throat.

Marissa curved one hand over her mouth and pressed the other to her stomach, as if she might be sick.

Without thinking, he pulled her against his chest and wound protective arms around her back. She curled against him and buried her face into her palms. Warmth and resolve blew through him in a powerful gale. "You're going to be okay. I'm going to see to it."

His phone buzzed, and Marissa stepped aside. A text message from West confirmed that a deputy was on his way with a print kit for the window.

Blake snapped a photo of Marissa's bed, then texted it to his team and brothers. They were going to need more than a print kit.

"Can you tell me if anything else was altered, missing or left behind?" He moved methodically through the room in search of something that could lead him to Nash.

Marissa scrutinized the room, moving slowly from closet to night stand and dresser before creeping softly toward the bed. "Just this," she whispered, as if she might wake the sleeping veil. "Why would he do this?"

"I don't know. Maybe he hoped to meet you back here." He regretted the words immediately and hated Nash all the more for the truth behind them.

Her eyes widened in horror. "Meet me back here for what?"

Blake's tongue seemed to swell as a line of horrific ideas presented themselves. Too many years on the job and in the military had irrevocably polluted his thoughts. Now, he saw danger everywhere.

Marissa backed away from the bed and freed a duffel bag from her closet. "He came here after I got away."

"Yes." Blake swallowed a brick of regret. *If only he'd shot Nash when he'd had the chance.*

"We were looking for him at the park, and he was here."

The words, *I'm sorry*, filled Blake's heart and mind, trapped behind a much stronger will to stay focused and do the job this time. Apologies could come when Marissa was safe and Nash was behind bars or dead. Preferably the latter for what he'd put her through.

Marissa filled the bag with clothes, opening and closing drawers, shoving handfuls of random items into the canvas duffel without looking.

Scents of powder and vanilla surrounded them, distracting Blake in dangerous and unprofessional ways. "We can wait outside in my truck." He scooped a pair of white lace panties up as they hit the floor beneath her gaping bag. He passed the soft scrap of material to Marissa, doing his best not to picture her in only those. "You don't have to stay in here with this." He tipped his head toward her bed.

She stuffed the panties into her bag and opened another drawer. "Thanks." Her cheeks reddened as their gazes locked.

"I'm going to check the perimeter."

"No." Alarm changed her features. "Don't."

"It's okay." Blake infused the words with as much promise as possible. "You're safe with me, and I'll make sure to keep you that way."

She dipped her chin and went back to stuffing things blindly into her bag.

Blake circled the home's exterior and returned to Marissa several minutes later. A fresh text had arrived. "The team secured a room for us at the Blue Ridge Lodge outside of town. We know now that you were targeted. That makes you safer with us until we find Nash, and we *will* find him."

She gnawed her bottom lip. "One room?"

"It'll be crowded but secure. My team and brothers will come and go as the investigation moves along. And don't worry, contrary to local legend, the Garrett men were raised to be gentlemen."

She pinned him with a fiercely ornery smile. "I was raised to be a princess. Look how that turned out. I'm about to spend the night with a man I just met."

He shot the ceiling another look and rearranged his ball cap. *If the job didn't kill him, protecting Marissa Lane might.*

MARISSA COULDN'T DROP the creepy sensation of being watched. Knowing a psychopath had been in her room had shaken her far worse than the attempted abduction. At least during the attack, she was aware of his presence, but he'd been inside her home. He'd been in her room. The contents of her overnight bag grew heavy on her lap. Had he looked inside her drawers? Touched her things? How long had he been planning to take her? How did he find her home? Endless questions ran rampant through her mind as she bounced on the passenger side of Blake's truck, feeling thoroughly violated.

Blake pulled into the parking spot beside a black town car at Blue Ridge Lodge and climbed out. He shook hands with a man in a gray suit standing outside the door to room one-eleven. They looked at Marissa through the windshield, mouths moving, eyes appraising.

She redirected her attention to the scenery. Blue

Ridge Lodge was gorgeous and nestled in the mountains where she'd practiced rock climbing and spelunking throughout high school. She'd long ago mastered the climbs and adventures the area had to offer, but back in the day, those hills were a great source of victory and self-confidence. If only she'd taken more photos of the excursions.

Blake lumbered toward the passenger door and pulled it open. "How are you holding up?"

She ducked her chin. "Okay."

Sympathy swam in his eyes. He moved away from the open door so she could climb down. "There's nothing we can do until the last of the divers arrive except keep you out of sight. The sheriff's department's on the lookout for Nash. My men are canvassing local hotels and campgrounds along with abandoned buildings and cabins. If Nash is still in Cade County, we'll find him."

Blake stole the duffel from her hand and hooked it over one broad shoulder. "Let's go inside. Neither of us have eaten since breakfast and that was one hell of a walk you took me on. Let me order dinner. We'll eat, and hopefully you can get a little rest while we're waiting on a new lead."

Marissa sank her teeth into the thick of her bottom lip and immediately released it. She was too late. Blake's gaze slid from her mouth to her eyes. He'd noticed her tell. He knew she was nervous. She could lie all day with her tongue, but she had no control over her face. "Okay. Dinner sounds good." As did a hot shower and fresh clothes. "Thank you."

She followed him inside the roomy junior suite. A small sitting area with a round table, chairs, couch and television were separated from the bedroom and en suite bath by a set of French doors. Marissa dragged her gaze away from the queen-size bed with notable effort. She told herself it was the fatigue in her bones that wanted her to head that way first, not the small tug in her belly that wondered if Blake preferred to be the big spoon or the little spoon.

He edged past her with the duffel and set it on the bed. "Burgers okay?"

She nodded too quickly, a sure sign of guilt. "Yeah. Good. Thank you. I'm going to shower." She snatched up the bag and hustled into the bathroom.

Safe behind the closed door, Marissa shed her dirty clothes and climbed into the steamy shower. Hot beads of water pounded against her tired, aching muscles, and she rubbed her eyes as the water ran over her face. The sensation did little to cleanse her mind of numerous inappropriate thoughts about Blake Garrett, the man who set her skin on fire with every smoldering look. She squeezed a dollop of shampoo onto her palm and worked her hair into a lather. Marissa was never plagued by so many inconceivable fantasies. The problem was obviously this awful day. Her emotions were too heightened to share a hotel room with that man. The excess adrenaline and fatigue were producing crazy thoughts. And why was there only one bed?

She rinsed the soap from her hair and body, clearing her skin and mind. There was no chemistry between she and Blake. She'd imagined his heated looks as a means of distraction, a psychological defense mechanism to deal with what had happened that morning. Clearly her subconscious assumed that if the hot FBI agent wanted her, then he'd protect her and she could feel safe.

She stepped onto the bath mat and wrapped a soft terry-cloth towel around her torso. Even if the looks Blake gave her were real, they didn't mean anything other than he was in possession of a libido. It was practically what the Garretts were known for. And so what? She rubbed her arms and legs vigorously with a second towel. Blake might want her. Short-term, of course. His family was single-minded and the whole town knew it. Married to the endless pursuit of justice. Addicted to the chase. Which was likely the reason Blake hadn't settled down. He probably wondered where the fun was in pairing up for life. Marissa expected that was where the fun really began, but what did she know?

She wound her hair into the second towel and rubbed a clear spot on the steamed-up mirror. Tears welled in her eyes at the sight of her bruised face and throat. Her heart pounded with fresh panic, as if Nash were still with her, pawing at her and looking at her and plotting to kill her if she didn't keep fighting. She swallowed a sob and turned to sit on the floor, back pressed to the door as tears streamed over her cheeks. No, this wasn't a day for finding love. This was a day best forgotten.

Thirty minutes later, Marissa dragged herself

from the bathroom, clean and dry. Her blond hair fell in soft piles over each shoulder, fluffy from the efforts of a complimentary dryer. She hadn't packed much makeup, but the lip gloss and mascara had helped her feel a little more human and less hideous despite the raging bruises along her jaw and throat.

Blake's body went rigid when he saw her.

The room was empty, save for a pair of white takeout bags on the little round table near the front window.

Marissa stared, unmoving. "What's wrong?"

Blake snapped into action, waving her closer to the table "Nothing. The final divers arrived while you were in the shower. My team went to meet them, but the sun's setting soon and they've postponed until morning. My guys are filling the divers in on what to look for and anything else they need to know. West and Cole have promised to keep me updated on their end." He settled into a red cushioned chair. "Now, we wait."

"Will I get to talk to your team when they come back?" She shifted her weight foot to foot. "Not that I plan to badger them or get in the way. I just wonder if I'll be exiled to the bedroom while you talk shop."

"We won't say anything that you can't hear."

Meaning they'd wait until she wasn't around to talk about the classified details, not that they'd be open with her about everything. She mulled that over. "Okay." She didn't love being excluded from any information so closely affecting her, but she had to trust Blake to do his job.

"I ordered burgers, fries and malts." His brows furrowed. "Do you eat this stuff?"

"Comfort food? Absolutely."

He unpacked the bag and set her burger and fries in front of her.

One whiff was all her body needed to recall its desperation for sustenance. She unraveled the butcher paper and chomped into her sandwich like a ravenous animal.

Blake watched her intently. "I'm feeling less guilty for that cruller. I suppose running five miles uphill before dawn seven days a week earns you plenty of room for burgers."

She sucked her straw flat, working a taste of chocolate malt into her mouth. "I've got good genes."

"The running doesn't hurt," he added. "You hike, bike, swim and scuba?"

"I leaned to scuba dive in college. I did crazy things then. I even tried parasailing and rock climbing." She chuckled. "I learned that I prefer to be on the ground."

He pushed a fry between smiling lips. "I've never done any of those things, and I've always thought of myself as an outdoorsman. You're raising the bar."

"You'll get used to it," she teased. "Adventuring is my job."

"Nature photography, right?"

She wiped her mouth and examined Blake's odd expression. "You look confused."

"I assumed you took pictures of wildflowers and butterflies."

She rolled her eyes and went in for another bite of burger. "I get up close and personal with nature. My photos are used for education. Last summer I photographed an eagle's nest on the summit. It was amazing."

Blake dropped his napkin on the table. "The summit? That's one hell of a dangerous climb." He furrowed his brows. "You must really love what you do."

"I do." She smiled. Another thing they had in common. It was no secret Blake loved his job. The pride practically oozed from him when he wore that badge.

Marissa sat back in her chair, allowing her head to roll and her muscles to relax. Slowly, her eyelids drooped shut. Blake cleared his throat, and she jumped. "What happened?"

He stood over her looking inexplicably sad. "You fell asleep sitting up."

"Oh." She checked the corners of her mouth for drool. "Sorry. I should go to bed." She stretched onto her feet, wincing at the pinch of tender muscles in her shoulders and neck.

Blake matched her move. "May I?" He motioned to the place where her hand rested on her bruised neck.

He waited for her to nod before stepping near.

Marissa braced herself to be touched by another towering man today. "Do they put you through medical training at the FBI?"

His warm fingers touched the tender skin of her throat and chin, tipping her head gently for a better look at the wounds. "A little. I think I got more experience growing up a Garrett." He snorted quietly. "At least one of us boys were in constant need of a cast or stitches for about ten years. Nearly drove my poor mom to drink."

Marissa smiled, though he couldn't see her from his new position at her back. She and Kara had been the same way, though their parents were often right beside them.

He circled back to face her. "These bruises are going to look a lot worse before they look better. I can get some ice in here if you want. That might help with swelling." He widened his stance until his face was nearly level with hers and shined a light in her eyes.

She swatted it away on instinct. "Where'd you get that."

"Pocket. Hold still and let me look."

"I don't have a concussion. I was attacked hours ago. I'm fine. Cole already checked. Remember?"

"You need to clean these abrasions."

"I did."

Blake straightened and cocked a brow. "When?"

"Bathroom. I never leave home without a first aid kit. The cuts are cleaned. They're already beginning to scab. I'm fine."

"That's what you keep saying. Did Cole offer to get a female medic to give you a more thorough evaluation?"

She sighed. "I'm. Fine. What happens to you now?

Will someone come to relieve you so you can go home and sleep?"

"I don't sleep much." He walked her to the bedroom and made a slow circuit through the room, peeking into the bathroom before returning to the doorway. "I'll wake you if anything significant happens."

Marissa dawdled, frightened by the prospect of being alone.

Her phone buzzed with a text.

Blake nodded toward the sound. "Tell your family I said everything's going to be okay." He pulled the door shut behind him as he left.

Marissa climbed into the waiting arms of a comfortable queen-size bed and rolled onto her back. She lifted her cell phone into view and swiped the screen to life. She didn't recognize the number on her new text message, but she opened it anyway.

Panic swelled in her chest and throat as she stared at the image of herself enveloped in Blake's strong arms. The photograph was clearly taken from outside her bedroom window only hours earlier.

And the message read, Consider this Agent Garrett's invitation to the wedding.

Chapter Four

The chair toppled behind Blake as he lunged toward the freshly closed French doors, the only things standing between him, Marissa and whatever had elicited her bloodcurdling scream. The barrier sucked open before he reached it, whipping suddenly inward to reveal his trembling charge.

"Blake." She choked on his name, extending her cell phone in his direction.

His gaze darted through the silent room behind her. No signs of an intruder. The window was securely closed. The bathroom door was open. No one was inside.

"Blake," she pleaded, wiggling the phone. "Take it."

Slowly, he holstered his sidearm. "You're alone."

"Yes."

His muscles unclenched by a fraction. He dragged his attention from her stricken face to the offering in her white-knuckled grip. He hadn't left her alone for more than thirty seconds. He'd barely pressed the straw of his chocolate malt to his lips before she'd screamed. The fine hairs along the back of his neck rose to attention as he pried the small pink device from her hand. *That scream.* His guts twisted at the thought of what it could have meant. What he could've found behind the doors.

"It's him," she whispered.

The momentary relief he'd felt at the sight of her was quickly replaced by the image on her screen. Revenge boiled in his blood. "This was the text you received?"

She nodded quickly, her attention glued to the phone.

He powered the device off and used his own to dial West's number. "We've got a new problem. Nash has Marissa's number. He sent a text with a photo. I don't know if he's tracked her. I powered the phone down. I'm pulling the SIM card now, but we need someone to capture prints outside her house and match them to the ones at the site of her attack. Also, get me a burner phone so she can stay in touch with her family." He disconnected and returned his focus to Marissa, the statue in baggy white pajamas.

Her attention remained wholly fixed on the phone. "I can't have it back?"

"Not right now."

"I have pictures on there."

"We won't remove anything personal from the device. I promise. I'm just keeping the card separate so Nash can't track us here."

Marissa's gaze snapped up to meet his. "He can do that?"

Twelve hours ago, Blake would've said no, but his opinion of Nash Barclay was rapidly changing. "Better not to take any chances."

She wrapped her arms around her middle and lifted her chin. "Okay."

"Why don't you get back in bed? Cover up. Try to rest."

Marissa cast a woeful look at the bed she'd no sooner climbed into than leapt back out of. "I could sleep on the couch." Her voice lifted on the final word, bringing a hopeful expression to her pinched brow. "Then you won't have to patrol both rooms."

Blake rocked back on his heels. Having her in his line of sight would make his job a lot easier, but after the day she'd had, and whatever Nash still had planned, a good night's sleep was best for Marissa. There was no way she'd get any decent rest on the couch. Not with local and federal authorities swarming in and out all night, trading intel and updates.

He dropped his chin an inch and cocked his head. "I'll be just fine. You take the bed. I'll keep watch." If it meant Marissa could rest, he'd make the extra effort.

"Or," she said softly, "you could work in here."

Maybe it was her voice. Maybe it was the tenderness in the offer, but something stirred in Blake's chest, extinguishing a tiny portion of the fire in his belly. His contempt for Nash had driven him this far, and he needed it now. What he didn't need was to think of the kind of work he could do in a room like that with a woman like her. Marissa had earned his respect before they'd ever met. She'd done what he couldn't do. When challenged by Nash, she'd gotten the best of him.

Blake stepped carefully into the front room of their suite and wedged the door open. "How about I set up shop here? If we leave this open, I can see the bed and the front door. You'll be safe, and I won't have to leave my post to check on you."

Marissa turned on her socked feet and went back to the bed. Whatever she thought of the offer, she didn't say, but she didn't argue either.

He flipped the light switch, casting her room into shadows, and went to drag the chair and table to its new location.

MARISSA WOKE WITH a start. Her fingers curled deep into the soft fabric of hotel bedsheets. Her limbs were heavy with fatigue and her mind groggy with the effects of a restless night. She pried her stinging eyes open and squinted against the streams of poorly filtered sunlight sneaking through closed hotel blinds. Thank goodness the night was over. She hadn't remembered falling asleep, but the dreams had come quickly. The rose petals and the lake. Nash and his song. She hadn't stopped running through the dark forest since the moment she'd closed her eyes.

In the dream, she didn't get away.

Blake flashed brilliant blue eyes on her in that moment, as if he'd somehow sensed her waking. "Morning." His easy southern drawl pulled her back to reality. He'd repositioned the table and chairs from the front room, and by the looks of him, sat guard all night.

He swiped a travel mug off the table and pushed onto his feet. He stopped at the doorway. "May I?"

She nodded, pressing her lips together, certain she needed a toothbrush or chewing gum before speaking to anyone.

A few unfamiliar faces turned her way, then back, immediately disinterested. The vibration of quiet voices electrified the air beyond her bedroom door, buoyed by the scent of black coffee and the outdoors.

Blake handed the cup to Marissa. "How are you feeling this side of yesterday?"

She bobbed her head in positivity. "Awful."

His mouth ticked up on one side. "Coffee helps."

She pressed the cup to her lips and sucked the steaming hot liquid. The burn on her tongue and scald on her throat were a necessary evil. There was no time to waste on letting the liquid cool. "What have we learned?"

"Not much. We've got your phone at the lab, and my men are comparing the prints at the lake with those outside your bedroom window." His voice drifted slightly off.

Was he recalling the stolen image as she was? The photo of her in his embrace? She could still feel the strength of his arms around her.

Marissa scooted upright in the bed, suddenly guilty for the comfort he'd forgone to keep her safe. "Didn't you sleep?" The question was rhetorical, its answer evident. The stubble on Blake's cheeks had darkened, nearly as much as the circles beneath his eyes. He hadn't changed clothes, and the shiny FBI badge he'd worn proudly around his neck when they met was now missing.

"As much as ever."

"You don't normally sleep?"

He flicked his attention to the bustle in the front room. "No."

"Hazard of the job?" she guessed.

"Something like that."

"Are you always on a case like this?" she wondered. Surely he wasn't always on call. "Do you get time off when you're done? Can you sleep then?"

He pursed his lips and turned piercing blue eyes back on her. "The cases close, but the people stick with me."

"I see." A piece of her heart broke for his. She couldn't imagine the things Blake had seen or how he put them aside when it was time to move on. "Will someone relieve you soon so you can at least try to rest?"

"I'm fine. I'll step outside and pull the door while you..." he circled one wrist "...do whatever ladies do in the morning."

Marissa pushed back the comforter and swung her legs over the bed's edge. "Normally I run, but I guess that's out of the question."

"Yep."

"I use the adrenaline to wake me up. I like the endorphin rush."

Blake pinned her with a cheeky smile. "Coffee's going to have to do today."

Marissa had never had much interest in photographing people, but she wouldn't mind taking a crack at Blake. His square jawline and brooding brow were more than print-worthy. The slight imperfection of his nose and faded scar above his temple were interesting too, but it was the protective edge, the palpable energy, that fascinated her most. Too many people were out for themselves these days, but Blake spent his life watching over others.

"What?" he rumbled, scanning the room around her.

"I was thinking that what you do is noble," she said, "and I'm wondering if anyone ever tells you that."

He snorted. "That's not one I've heard before. No."

"That's too bad." Marissa stretched onto her feet and reached for the ceiling. Her bunched and exhausted muscles complained at the effort. "Well, if I can't run, what am I doing today?" She dropped her hands together at her waist. "Another trip to the lake? Maybe down to the station?"

"I'm headed to the station to see what the team's got down there," he said, pointing a finger at his chest. "You're going to stay here with your detail. I won't be long." He fished a small black cell phone from his pocket and set it on the nightstand. "This is ready for use. We'll get your personal device back to you as soon as tech's done with it. They're going to run a few more diagnostics first."

"Thank you." Marissa hurried into the attached bathroom and shut the door. "When are you leaving for the station?" she yelled.

She discarded her pajamas and shoved her legs into the soft jeans she'd set out the night before.

"Soon," he replied. "Take your time. If I'm not here when you get back…"

She pulled the door open with one hand and brushed her teeth with the other.

"Whoa." Blake stepped back. "What are you, Houdini?"

She'd dressed hastily in her chosen outfit and raked a brush through her hair, still slightly damp from last night's shower. Marissa lifted a finger into the air and turned to the sink to rinse her mouth. "You're not leaving without me."

"There's nothing you can do right now," he said, drifting closer to the open bathroom door. "My goal is to keep you safe and out of sight." His gaze slid over the multicolored bruising on her cheek, jaw and throat.

Her hand went to the aching spots on instinct. She'd tried not to look too long at her battered reflection when she'd driven a lip gloss wand along her bottom lip. The thick line across her cheekbone hurt, but it was nothing like the infernal sting where her face had collided with the tree, leaving heavy rows of scratches from the tree's bark.

"I'm coming." She grabbed a hooded sweatshirt

from her bag on the floor and pulled the strings until welts left by Nash's fingers were no longer visible. The marks had raised and darkened overnight, leaving distinct imprints of his hands like shadows clasped around her throat. She didn't need everyone she saw today looking at her the way Blake was looking at her now.

Blake stepped into the doorway, blocking her view of the small crowd in the suite's front room. He searched her top to bottom with cautious eyes before lingering his gaze on her cheek. "You sure?"

"Yeah."

He stepped aside, opening one arm to direct her out. "We'll take my truck to the station. West says the sketch artist will be there soon. He was bringing her to you, but I'll let him know there's no need."

"A sketch artist?" Marissa grabbed the new phone from her nightstand. "I didn't see the face of the man who grabbed me."

"Anything you can tell her will help. I know this is Nash, but I need more than my gut to prove I'm right. Tell her what you remember, and whatever it is, it'll be enough."

"I don't see how."

Blake stopped to retrieve his badge and sidearm from the table. He signed his name to something, then whisked her out the door and into the cab of his truck.

"Last chance," he said, slipping the shifter into Reverse. "You can still stay if you'd like. There's lots of qualified personnel who could look out for you in there. West can still bring the sketch artist up here."

"No. It's good for me to get out. I feel like a sitting duck in there."

"Fair enough." Blake guided his truck away from the hideout and down the winding country road back to town.

Warm autumn winds rattled the trees and speckled the pavement with brightly colored leaves. It was hard to believe something as ugly as Nash Barclay could exist in a place as beautiful and peaceful as this one. Harder still to believe Nash wanted her. What had she done to gain his attention? How close was he to finding her again?

Blake stared at Marissa as he took the next right. "You look ready to jump."

She loosened her grip on the seat's edge. "I usually run to blow off steam. Now, I've got more to worry about than I ever have and no way to work out the tension." Her cheeks heated as numerous ideas for burning energy with Blake came to mind. "How do you do it?" she asked, desperate to redirect the images in her mind. Another minute of those thoughts, and she'd need to crack a window for air.

Blake lifted and dropped one shoulder. "I run."

"You run?" A smile broke over her face. "Really?"

"Well, don't act so surprised. I don't do it in the wilderness or up a cliff at five a.m. like you, but yeah. I run."

Marissa faced forward, her smile set in place. She could feel his eyes on her cheek. There was no logical reason for the pleasure coursing through her, but the fact they shared a hobby made her happy.

"When you grow up with three younger brothers, like I did, you'll do anything for an hour alone."

What would life have been like for Marissa with two more little sisters?

"It was always just Kara and me. We did everything with our folks. You think I'm outdoorsy. You should meet my family. Especially Kara. She's a leaf on the wind. She never stops moving, and she only comes inside when she has to."

"I'd love to meet them someday."

Marissa turned to face Blake. She'd like that, too, and she knew why. Dumb as it was, she liked Blake's company a little too much. But why would he want to meet her family? She examined the lines around his eyes and mouth for signs he was joking, or lying. Though, she had no idea how to tell the latter.

She turned her eyes back to the road with an internal groan. Blake was a nice guy and a good agent who was just doing his job. He probably said whatever he thought would make the people in his care feel most at ease.

She had to admit he was good. At his side, it was easy to forget they were in danger.

A little while later, Blake held the door as Marissa entered the bustling station. She recognized the members of her local sheriff's department. She'd grown up with most of them in one capacity or another. The FBI agents were easy enough to identify as well. Though she only knew Blake, the agents were dressed in slacks and jackets like the ones Blake had on when they'd met.

Small groups of official-looking men and women huddled around every desk, discussing the scattered contents of file folders or taking a call on speaker-phone. Marissa's name was on the lips of a dozen local protectors at once.

Blake's warm palm slid against the small of her back and nudged her forward.

"Sorry." She hadn't realized she'd stopped moving.

West stood in the hallway, stirring a cup of coffee and frowning. His gaze locked on Marissa's throat.

She adjusted the hooded sweatshirt, but his eyes simply moved north and stuck to the abrasions on her cheek.

"Blake, Marissa." He nodded. "Can I get you any-thing?"

"No." She cleared her throat to sound more con-fident than she felt.

"All right, then let's get started."

BLAKE FOLLOWED WEST into the thick of the crowd where a half-dozen men and women handed him files and reports. He flipped through the slew of in-formation looking for something to prove the man he was after was the same one who'd gotten away from him five years ago.

Marissa took a seat at the desk's edge and watched the group. Her head moved back and forth with each new voice, following every word. Blake could prac-tically hear the line of questions compiling for their drive home. He grimaced. Not *home*. Back to the hotel where they were staying *because she was a victim in need of protection.*

"This is everything from the traffic cams?" he asked, turning a few grainy photos toward West.

"No. Those are everything we have from the surveillance camera outside the bank. We don't have traffic cams or face recognition software, hell, half the town still comes to the library to use the internet. We're lucky to have those shots."

"Right." Blake rubbed his burning eyes. "So, we think he drives a pickup."

A deputy nodded. "An unfamiliar pickup was spotted outside the northern forest gates around the same time Miss Lane flagged down the man who drove her here. We asked around about the truck, and when we learned it was seen on Main Street, we contacted the bank to review the footage."

"Thanks." Blake gave the picture a careful examination. The entire windshield was in shadow, probably the worst photo he'd ever seen. He couldn't even see the grill from that angle, let alone a license plate.

He clenched and released a frustrated fist at his side. Marissa lifted her gaze from his hand to his eyes. She didn't miss anything.

"Agent Garrett?" A woman in jeans and a *Doctor Who* T-shirt jogged up the aisle in his direction, bobbing between desks and around staring agents. "I'm Cora from tech. I came in as soon as they called. I've been here all night. Sorry about the..." she motioned to her outfit, then shook her head and continued. "I traced the text back to a burner phone. The phone was left on and dropped in a trash receptacle outside the national park. We recovered the phone. No prints, but it's a really basic phone."

"That's not a surprise," he said. "People don't buy basic phones for personal use. They want bells and whistles. Criminals buy basic so they can use them for something like this." He turned his attention back to the stack of useless intel gathered on the desk.

"Agent Garrett," Cora continued.

He dragged his most polite expression out and waited.

"I called every store in Cade County selling phones like the one we found. Most said they'd check their inventory against the stock and let me know. The guy at the truck stop diner on Deer Run Road said he sold a phone like this yesterday at three o'clock. He remembered the time because it was the end of his shift. The man paid with cash, but the truck stop has a camera watching the register."

Blake's spine went rigid. A spike of hope rammed through him. "Tell me he's sending a picture of the man who bought that phone."

"Yes, sir."

"How soon?"

"Anytime. He's looking through the footage now."

West leaned against the corner of the desk beside Blake. "Maybe take a load off until we hear something new," he suggested, spinning an unopened bottle of water in his palm like an Old West gunslinger. “You’re so tired you can barely stand there without swaying.”

“He didn’t sleep,” Marissa tattled.

“Wait,” West said. “Why don’t you put a pin in the nap and take a shower first. Isn’t that what you had on yesterday?”

Blake snatched the bottle from West’s hand and cracked the lid open. “Thanks, I’m fine.” He took long deep pulls on the liquid, realizing then that he’d become dry as the desert.

West fanned a hand in front of his nose. “Feel free to splash some of that on you if you want to.”

Blake finished the bottle and walked away from the crowd. West followed. Blake shot a look over his shoulder, where Marissa continued to watch from her seat. “He could’ve killed her.”

“But he didn’t,” West said, not missing a beat. “She’s tough, and she’s smart, and he didn’t get her.”

Blake nodded. He’d give Marissa that. She was one of a kind. “If he had, it would’ve been on me.”

West crossed his arms and locked Blake in his steady gaze. “He didn’t, and it’s not.”

“Agent Garrett?” Cora’s voice carried through the stream of white noise.

The Garretts moved instantly toward her. “What do you have?” Blake asked.

“I just heard from the truck stop, and it looks like we’ve got a match.” She turned the large digital tablet in her hands to face them, and Marissa gasped.

"That's him," Marissa pointed, moving to join them in the room's center. "That's the man from the lake this summer."

Chapter Five

West marched forward, holding the digital image above his head to face the other officials. His voice boomed through the instantly silent room. “This is Nash Barclay. Get his name and face on every news channel this side of the Mississippi, and we need it done now. Right now. Talk to bus terminals and the highway patrol. He might be driving an old Ford pickup, plates unknown. We want sightings only, no civilian apprehension attempts. He’s dangerous. Drive that point home.”

The room scrambled into action.

Marissa caught Blake’s sleeve in her fingertips. “It’s him?”

“It’s him,” Blake answered.

An uncomfortable mix of fear and victory beat through her. She’d hoped Blake was wrong, that some other, less murderous man had grabbed her, but at least now Nash couldn’t hide. Not with his face splashed across the nightly news and morning papers.

Blake’s attention traveled to her hand on his sleeve

before reconnecting with her eyes. “I guess you don’t need to meet with the sketch artist.”

“Right.” She released him in favor of cradling her torso. “I didn’t think I remembered his face, but that’s definitely it.” She tightened her arms around her middle, thankful to be at the sheriff’s department when a known serial killer was running around. A sliver of guilt wiggled through her. Not everyone was as safe as she was, surrounded by federal agents and local law enforcement officials. Another woman could be next. There were plenty of twentysomething blondes to keep Nash entertained. In fact, she had a sister who looked a lot like her.

Marissa pulled her phone from her pocket and gave Blake an uneasy look. “I’m going to call Kara and tell her to stay in today.” Hopefully Kara didn’t need the advice. Maybe she’d taken the news of Marissa’s attack to heart and planned a quiet day at home.

“Hello?” Kara’s voice trilled through the speaker.

A whoosh of relief swept from Marissa’s lungs. Kara was fine. “Hey, it’s me. Thought I’d check in.”

“Oh, hey!” The smile in her sister’s voice was contagious. “Why didn’t you call before bed last night? I was worried. Your phone was off. Where are you calling from? Did you get a new number?” Wind battered the speaker. Marissa’s attention jumped to Blake’s waiting face.

“No. Kara? Where are you?”

“Hiking. Why? Do you want to meet for breakfast? I packed a good one.”

"I can't. I'm sorry. Listen, I need you to go home, or to Mom and Dad's. Stay there today, okay? They've identified my attacker."

"Is it him? The fugitive you said they were looking for?"

Marissa nodded, knowing Kara couldn't see, but finding the words impossible.

"Holy crap," Kara whispered. Marissa's silence must have been enough of an answer.

"He's still out there," Marissa warned.

She thought she saw Blake wince, but his blank agent face was in position when she gave him a closer look. "Please be safe," she continued to Kara. "I'll call again as soon as I know something. Tell Mom and Dad I'm safe. I'm staying with the authorities for now."

Kara swore. "I'll head straight there from here."

"Thank you." Marissa's eyes stung as she disconnected with her sister. "She's safe," she told Blake. "I sent her to our parents' house."

"Good. Why don't you let me take you back to the hotel now?"

"No," she blurted. "I'm okay here. I'm obviously safe, and you have things to do. I won't get in the way. I can wait in the break room again."

"Agent Garrett?" A man in a gray suit waved one hand overhead. His jacket parted in the front to reveal the FBI badge anchored to his sleek black belt. "We're needed at the lake."

"Take me." Marissa's hand snapped out to catch Blake's. "Please."

Blake ignored her. "What's going on?"

The man gave Marissa a long look. "They say they found something. We need to get up there."

Blake pulled his hand free from Marissa's grip. Before she could protest the rejection, he pressed those same warm fingers to the small of her back. "Let's go."

THE DRIVE TO the lake was a blur. Partially due to Marissa's hazy thoughts and morbid fears, partially as a result of Blake's speed. The silence was palpable in the warm cab. Blake stole looks at her from the corner of his eye, but kept whatever he was thinking to himself. She wished he'd just spit it out. The silence crawled all over her skin like a nest of baby spiders. He might be calm and focused under this kind of pressure, but the worry was eating her alive.

The vehicle slowed as a pair of rangers came into view near the park entrance. A line of reporters yammered into microphones along the roadside, just outside the gate, using a Cade County National Forest and Road Closed sign as the backdrop to their story.

Blake flashed his badge, and the rangers motioned him to pass. The looks on the uniformed men's faces suggested they knew more than Blake or Marissa, and it wasn't good.

The truck rocked to a stop in the grass between two black vans marked Cade County Coroner. Blake released his belt and turned on the seat to face Marissa. "I don't know what we're walking into, but I'm guessing it's going to be rough. I want to remind you that you don't have to be here. It's not too late to return to the hotel or go back to the station."

Marissa's tongue stuck to the roof of her mouth and sweat pooled in her palms. The coroner's vans weren't there by accident. She didn't want to see what the divers had found, but where else would she go? To a hotel room with a carousel of uniformed strangers all looking at her like she might break? Like she was a victim. No. She'd stay with Blake. At least with him, there was no judgement. He had other things on his mind, and she appreciated the room to feel however she wanted without those probing, curious looks.

"I'll stay," she said. She reached for her door, and Blake followed suit, rushing around the truck's hood to meet her.

"You don't need to be brave." He moved into a broad shaft of sunlight with his jaw clenched, the expression flush with concern.

Marissa inhaled a steadying breath. She squared her shoulders, determined to be as honest as possible with a man whose mere presence seemed to put her at ease. "I'm not brave. I'm scared to death. I don't want to be here any more than you want me here, but this is just the way it is. I want to be with you."

Blake yanked his chin back. "What?"

She sank her teeth into the thick of her bottom lip. She hadn't meant the words the way they'd sounded, but could she deny them? He was rugged and handsome with a voice like molasses, and the man was nothing if not attentive. She blew out a slow breath as her mind began to wander.

Blake waited, hip cocked, gaze delving into hers, as if he could pull the thoughts from her head.

"Until this is over," she clarified, taking interest in a nearby tree and ignoring the warmth in her belly. She shored herself up and met his gaze once more. "The way I see it, this entire situation is horrible. There's no silver lining. No good angle. It's awful, and it's ugly, but I don't see how he can get to me again as long as I'm with you. So, I'm staying."

MARISSA'S POSTURE WAS RIGID, something she did to appear bigger, Blake assumed. Though, he hadn't thought of her as small since she'd first opened her mouth to tell him how he was going to handle her case. Being pocket-size required a person to apply themselves more assertively. He'd never thought much of that fact before meeting her. He'd passed six foot by junior year in high school. Being overlooked or underestimated had never been his problem.

Until Blake had met Nash, he hadn't had a lot of problems. Now, he had two major ones. Catching the sonofagun who'd eluded him for five years, and protecting the woman in front of him who was doing her best not to look nearly as frightened as she truly was. The second task would be a lot easier if she hadn't just announced her intent to stay under his thumb. Not only would her constant presence make it impossible for him to go hunting for his nemesis, it also made Blake vulnerable. Marissa was a distraction.

She'd been slowly making mud of his clarity with those big blue eyes and endless bravado, and every minute he wasted worrying about her was time Nash gained on him.

Worse still, and ridiculous as it was, Blake wanted her with him. He'd promised to keep her safe, and he wasn't the kind of man who broke his word. "Fine." He set his hand against the small of her back once more, a frustrating habit he'd developed and couldn't seem to shake. Normally, he maintained a strict no-touching policy for those in his charge, but this was different. The added connection was a comfort to her. At least that was what he'd told himself when she didn't swat him away the first time he made the move. Not that he'd planned it. Reaching for her had come naturally, another thing that had surprised him. "You can stick with either of my brothers while I work. They'll keep you safe, and you can trust them."

"I know, and I do."

They moved toward the lake in unison, becoming the center of attention as those already on scene noticed their arrival. A man in a wet suit leaned his backside against a tree, hands on knees, eyes closed. Blake's gut fisted. He knew that deep breathing technique. If the diver hadn't been sick yet, he was about to be.

"Blake." A familiar and commanding voice caught Blake's attention and turned him around. His father tromped through the tall grasses at the lake's edge wearing fatigues and waders.

Blake smiled, and led Marissa toward the grasses. He hadn't seen his dad in nearly a year, but it was eerily like looking in a mirror. One that told the future anyway.

"Here's another one you can trust," Blake told Marissa. "This is my dad, Martin Garrett. Dad, this is Marissa Lane."

Marissa raised her small hand to him. "Sheriff Garrett. It's nice to meet you."

His dad stepped free of the water and accepted her offer with a sad smile. "I'm sorry to hear about what happened to you yesterday."

"Thank you, sir."

"You're a brave woman."

She pursed her lips and looked away.

Blake's dad pinned him with a pointed look. "Did they tell you what they found down there?"

"Not yet, but I don't suppose they had to." The somber feel in the air, coupled with the coroner's vans, could mean little else.

"Probably not." His dad sighed the words. Twenty years as the local sheriff had worn him down. He'd spearheaded West's landslide campaign. It was time, he'd said, to get to know his family again. Let another Garrett take the reins for a while.

"Look," Marissa whispered.

Bubbles floated and burst on the lake's smooth surface, sending ripples through the reflections of Marissa, Blake and his father. A heartbeat later, two divers' heads broke free. Together, they towed a body to shore.

His father groaned.

Marissa stepped behind Blake. Her fingers

pressed against his side, either for protection or balance, he couldn't be sure. When he'd moved between her and the reporter, she'd rejected the shielding. He didn't blame her now. No one should see what he was watching. It shouldn't be happening.

Her ragged breaths blew against his shirt. She was probably thinking the same thing he was. That body could have been her.

"Dad?" Blake said, turning for a look at his lifelong hero.

"Yep." The town's former sheriff and eternal protector slid an arm around Marissa's shoulders. "Why don't we give these folks some room to work."

Blake waited as his father led Marissa several yards away, then headed for the divers as they arranged the exhumed body carefully on a sheet set out by the county coroner. Drops of water fell from their suits onto her pale, swollen face and tattered wedding gown.

Blake pulled his eyes away with a curse. "Was she alone?"

"No, sir." One diver answered as the other strode away on unsteady legs. "Five more," he added in the detached monotone of a man in shock.

"Five?" Blake cast his gaze over the bubbling water. That couldn't be right. "Nash had four victims in total. You're saying there were six bodies down there?"

A pair of men in blue windbreakers edged Blake and the diver away from the woman. "Excuse us." They stretched another sheet beside the first.

And another beside that.

With six sheets spread along the peaceful lake's edge, the men in windbreakers returned to the woman and went to work immediately, examining her eyes, nose and mouth, cleaning under her nails and probing her skin with blue medical gloves.

Blake rubbed a heavy hand through his hair and gripped the back of his neck.

Two new divers appeared on the water's surface, towing another woman dressed in white. The veil from her hair sank slowly in the water behind them.

The bodies kept coming, just as the first diver had said, delivered by the hands of men and women who'd undoubtedly retrieved many others from similar fates, but never, he guessed, had anyone there seen anything like this. The rescuers' faces were as white as the victims. They bumbled onto shore stricken, ill and rattled.

Blake watched with disbelieving eyes as the women were lined up and examined in the warm autumn sun. It was a juxtaposition that turned his stomach. Six women. *Six.* How had he missed two victims? He'd dedicated himself to knowing this case. He knew the victims. Had met with their families. Internalized their devastating losses. How could he have missed not one but two victims?

West's men met each diver as they finished their duty and led them aside. They'd need to give an account of what they'd seen down there.

Blake walked the space between five occupied sheets, studying the disfigured faces and patchy hair. Years underwater had all but removed their identities. Aside from their families, and the animal who did this, Blake was probably the only one who'd recognize them. "Marcia Gold," he told the men working on the first body. "Angela Olmstead," he said to the next. "Jessica Snow. Monica Knisely."

He stopped beside the fifth body where a woman wearing an ID badge from the medical examiner's office tucked wads of loose hair into an evidence bag. "What happened to her?" he asked. The body was grotesquely misshapen, portions missing. Her gown was nearly torn to shreds by age and the lake's ecosystem.

The M.E. labeled the bag and set it into her case. "This one's been down there a while. Longer than the others. Maybe by as much as a year."

"A year." The words warbled off Blake's tongue. "Are you sure?"

She offered a patient smile. "It'll take longer to identify her, if we can. There's a lot of damage here, but we'll know more soon, and we'll get the facts to you the moment we have them." The woman stretched onto her feet and patted his shoulder.

A hush rolled over the crowd behind them, on the heels of splashing water. The sixth body had made it to the surface.

Blake hung his head as he turned to see what new atrocity awaited. Would it be another woman murdered *years* ago? Someone else who he had no clue existed? Would this have been Marissa's fate if she weren't so fierce and determined?

"Blake." Marissa's voice sounded nearby, closer

than he'd expected, but he couldn't force his eyes from the lake.

The final two divers rushed forward with a woman who couldn't have been underwater more than a few weeks. She was blonde and blue-eyed like the others, petite and dressed in a long-sleeved wedding gown.

Blake's chest tightened. The weight of too many sleepless nights and five years of self-loathing pressed the air from his lungs. Anger boiled in his gut. He could've stopped this five years ago and he didn't. Now someone else was dead. Another life taken. Because of him.

West strode into view, cell phone pressed to his ear. "I need the missing persons report on Annie Linz. Twenty-something jogger. Went missing near the county line early this month." He knelt beside the young woman and turned her face carefully toward him, then fell back on his haunches. He cast a look over one shoulder and dipped his chin at Blake.

The ground tilted beneath Blake. Nash had killed again and he'd had no idea. Everything he'd thought he knew about this case had gone out the window the moment he'd arrived home at the summons of a madman, which he realized was exactly what had happened. Nash could've killed anywhere, but he'd come back to Blake's hometown. It probably also wasn't a fluke that Marissa got away. Nash wanted to be hunted. He'd probably let her win that fight, and he'd used her to send the message right to Blake's ear.

"Blake." Marissa's voice was closer now, and

more desperate. She fell against him with hands over her eyes. The impact sent him back a step. She buried herself against his side. "I was wrong. I can't be here. Please, take me away."

His chest ached as he pulled himself away from all those women he couldn't save and focused on the one he still could. In fact, he was slowly coming to realize that he'd do anything to protect Marissa from anyone who tried to hurt her again, and that truth had nothing to do with his job. "Okay. Let's go."

MARISSA FOLLOWED BLAKE through the crowd and away from the ghastly scene. She sucked lungfuls of air, desperate not to be sick. Whatever she'd expected to come out of the lake, that wasn't it. "I'd hoped they'd found some small piece of evidence," she said, choking back her fear. "I wanted the coroner vans to be a precaution, not a necessity. Did you see the last woman? She looked like me." She covered her mouth again to stop the rambling.

"They all did at one point," Blake said. He watched for her response. "Nash has a type, and you're it."

She did her best not to overreact. Was there an overreaction to what he'd just said? Blake probably thought so, and she didn't want to be labeled as baggage. He could exile her to the hotel room where she'd have no idea what was going on or if she was in danger again. She wasn't sure if that scenario was worse than playing witness to the things she'd seen today, but both were scary. Given the choice, she'd rather be afraid with Blake than without him.

He pinched the bridge of his nose.

"Are you okay?" she asked, recalling his expression at the sight of the women being extracted from the lake.

"I'm fine."

He wasn't. She could see it in his eyes. He'd aged in those last few minutes by the lake.

She'd watched him as a gauge. Was this normal to him? To the other officials? It wasn't. Everyone had looked the way she felt. Some of the divers were physically sick while being interviewed. This thing that was happening in her town was absolutely sinister, and she was caught in the center of it.

Marissa leaned against a tree to tie her shoe and pull herself together. "Maybe you should get some sleep when we get back to the hotel."

"I'm fine." The words were resolute, from the mouth of a man who'd clearly repeated them a thousand times.

"Your eyes are rimmed in red. I doubt you slept at all last night, and I know you haven't eaten today." West had made a similar assessment when Blake arrived at the sheriff's department yesterday. So his poor self-care wasn't just about the last twenty-four hours. It was something more. How long had he been this way?

He turned his suddenly heated gaze on her.

"Don't say you're fine," she warned.

"I am."

She snorted. "You're predictable. I'll give you that." She pushed off the tree and continued down the path toward the parking lot, in no hurry to get back to her new reality.

Blake fell into step, easily matching his long stride to her much shorter one. "I'm sorry you had to see that. No one should have."

"Do you think that he was dragging me toward the lake yesterday?" she asked. "That he had his gear ready to go? Was that why we found the scuba weights in the grass?"

"I don't know."

"Where do you think he gets the dresses?"

Blake didn't answer. "There's a lot I don't know these days."

The trail ended too soon, dumping them back at the crowded lot. Official vehicles peppered the space between those she presumed belonged to the divers.

Blake's truck was still sandwiched between coroner's vans. Marissa marched to the passenger door, careful not to think too long about what she'd seen at the lake.

Blake leaned over his hood and plucked a sheet of paper from beneath his windshield wiper. A slew of curses poured from his lips, and he pulled his phone from his pocket. "Get in." He unlocked the truck doors and pointed at Marissa. "West?" he barked into the phone. "I've got contact." He pressed the paper facedown on the window and turned in a small circle, examining the quiet forest around him. "There was a picture on my truck. Probably the next victim. We need a name and address. We've got to get to her before he does."

Marissa climbed inside and locked her door. Her gaze swept to the photo staring at her through the arching glass. A boulder of fear landed on her chest, obstructing her airways and aching in her throat. "Blake!"

The driver's door jerked open. "What?" He leaned over the seat, eyes wide. "What happened?"

She fumbled for her phone with weak, uncoordinated hands. Her tear-blurred gaze jumped to the photo on his windshield. "That's my sister."

Chapter Six

Marissa worked her fingers over the phone screen, dialing Kara as quickly as possible with shaking hands. Blake's voice boomed beside her in the truck cab as he contacted West and his team. His words were lost as Marissa counted the rings. Had they always been so long and far between? "Voice mail," she whispered.

The truck rumbled to life and reversed through the grass and gravel with a loud roar. Stones blew out behind them, clanging and rattling against the fenders and undercarriage as they spun for the gate.

Marissa's ears rang. "She didn't pick up." *Why* didn't she pick up? Marissa dialed again.

The truck jumped between a tree and the guard gate, not bothering to stick to the road or wait for the removal of the barricade. "There's a deputy en route to Kara's house," Blake said, tearing up the road at nearly double the posted thirty-five miles per hour speed limit. He pressed a button on his dash and a red glow flashed over his windshield, presumably from the unit on the truck's roof.

"Voice mail." Marissa hung up and dialed again.

A news van gave chase in Marissa's side view mirror. It was no wonder with the exit they'd made.

Blake cursed and jammed his finger against the touchscreen on his dash. "Dial West," he ordered.

Marissa's head swam and her tummy churned. Blake's voice became the backdrop to her fear as he explained the new situation to West and set plans to beat Nash to Kara. Assuming he didn't already have her.

Nash Barclay could have anything he wanted, except Kara. Marissa would trade anything she had for her sister. Including herself. The voice mail picked up again, and Marissa slammed the phone onto the bench beside her.

"Hey." Blake lowered a hand over hers, trapping her shaky fingers in his steel grip. "Breathe."

Marissa pulled in a long, shuddered breath and released it. Blake's presence was a tonic to her nerves, but his touch was so much more. She gripped his strong fingers, allowing them to syphon her fear and stall the erratic pounding in her chest. His broad palm engulfed her small hand, covering it with his protection and sending sparks of electricity over her skin. She refocused on the road. "Turn right on Main and head for Blue Grass Run. She's the yellow one-story at the top of the hill. There's a tree in the yard with a swing and window boxes on the sills." Marissa's voice cracked. Her sister was too sweet and kind to fall victim to a monster.

"Got it." He released her hand to jam the horn on his steering wheel before running a red light.

Cool air rushed over her fingers in the absence of his grip, and immediate disappointment set in. "I know Blue Grass Run," he said. "It's a nice neighborhood, and that's good news. There are probably people outside today. Kids playing. Dogs walking. Witnesses. Plus, if she's anything like you, then she's smart, and you've told her what's going on. She won't answer the door to a stranger or invite anyone inside."

That was all true, but Marissa hadn't invited Nash into her house either, and he'd been there just the same. Pawing through her things, lingering at the window. Photographing her with Blake.

She let out a ragged breath and dialed Kara again. *Voice mail.*

Blake drove onto the curb outside Kara's house a few minutes later. Marissa hit redial.

"Wait here." Blake locked her in the truck and walked through the yard to meet Cole and another agent at Kara's porch.

"Come on," Marissa whispered to her phone. When she hung up this time, she dialed her parents. Kara was probably already there. She'd probably just forgotten her phone in the car or left it on the couch while she helped their mom in the kitchen. Kara was sweet, but she was naive and a bit clueless, never really seeing the big picture. She was fun, but unintentionally reckless and as hopelessly self-absorbed as any twenty-one-year-old who'd never had a true reason to worry.

"Hello?" Her mother answered on the first ring.

"Mama?"

"Marissa? Where are you? Are you okay?"

"I'm fine. Is Kara with you?" she asked. "We're at her place now. She's not here, but I told her to wait with you and she said she would."

"She's on her way," her mom answered.

"Oh, thank goodness."

"Marissa," she whispered. "Have you seen the news?"

"Yes." The word floated from her lips like a ghost from her worst nightmare. She'd seen the news and much worse this morning. The last woman pulled from the lake could've easily been her or Kara. Blake hadn't even known Nash was back at it until Marissa had gotten away from him yesterday.

Her gaze drifted back to the men on Kara's porch, and the world spun. The trio of oversized lawmen had shifted their positions, revealing a previously shielded stack of old-fashioned suitcases beside Kara's door. The pile was topped with a wedding veil.

The luggage was posed as if waiting for a photograph.

Or a honeymoon.

Marissa said a hasty goodbye to her mother, and tried not to be sick. She gripped the door handle, debating whether or not to jump out and join the men. Questions flooded her mind, but Blake had told her to stay put. She chewed her thumbnail and watched as Blake moved methodically around the perimeter of her sister's home, running his fingers along the window and door frames, like he had at her place, while curious neighbors looked on. Cole and a member of Blake's team hauled the cases away with blue-gloved hands.

Tears of fear welled in her eyes. What did this mean?

The door locks popped and Blake swung himself in beside her. "Have you found her?" he asked.

Marissa nodded. "She's headed to my parents'. Can we go there? I need to see her."

"Yes, ma'am." He folded himself behind the wheel and started the truck, a measure of relief in his brow. "No signs of forced entry. You saw the cases?"

"Yes." She watched for his reaction, but his expression was painfully blank. "Nash delivered the luggage?"

"I think so, yes, but it only means that he's playing with us, nothing more. Once we have Kara, we'll assign her a detail." He shot Marissa a pointed look. "This is going to be okay."

Marissa felt her brows grind together. "How can you say that?"

The news van that had attempted following them from the national park turned onto Kara's street and motored toward them.

"Because I won't accept any other outcome." Blake powered down his window as they drew near. He hung his elbow over the open window when the van stopped beside him in the street. "Deputy Garrett is patrolling this street with a federal agent. Someone reported a sighting of Nash Barclay. I'm headed back to the park to see if anything else has happened there."

The stunned news van driver bobbed his head. "Thank you."

Blake powered his window up and pressed gently on the gas pedal.

The van sat in the road for several long beats as Blake's truck rolled away. He snuck glances in his rearview mirror until the van sprang to life and headed for his brother and teammate.

Marissa turned on her seat for a better look out the back window. The fear of betrayal burned in her chest. Surely Blake wouldn't have given a reporter more information than he'd shared with her. Would he? "Was that true about Nash?"

"No. I lied about the Nash spotting to give the reporter a reason to stay here instead of following us to your parents' house. Cole has already bagged the evidence and put it out of sight. Let him deal with the reporter."

She swiveled back in relief. "What did you say Cole and the other agent are doing?"

"They're canvassing." Blake gave her a quick look. "It's due diligence to let her neighbors know he's out there. Educated civilians have stopped more than one killer. They'll be assets, keeping watch on her house and property. We'll broadcast the same message for vigilance on the nightly news, but one-on-one contact is better. People get desensitized.

Knocking on their doors is a call to action. It makes them accountable."

Marissa nodded, eager now for her childhood home, and bubbling with the need to be with Kara and her parents. "I guess you get to meet my family after all."

Blake's lips curved slightly, and the small smile reached his eyes. "See, the day's looking up already."

She matched his easy expression. "Family's important to you." That made one more thing to like about Blake Garrett. Not that she was counting. Her dad would appreciate it, too. "Nothing trumps family" was practically her dad's motto.

Blake exhaled with an infinitesimal shake of his head. "Family's everything." He gave her a curious look before dropping the smile.

Marissa straightened in her seat and adjusted the belt, trying not to wonder too much about what that look had meant, or if Blake was making light of those suitcases when they were really something much worse. "Thank you."

"For what?"

"Everything. For keeping me safe and calm. For watching out for my sister."

He crawled to a stop at the red light before speaking. "My job is to protect people." The gravelly tone in his voice made her think there was more he wanted to say, but as usual, he didn't.

Marissa folded her hands in her lap and turned her face to the widow at her side. She'd almost forgotten the big picture. This wasn't about her. Blake's attentiveness and the things he was doing for her weren't personal. They were in his job description.

THE LANE HOME was bigger than Blake had expected, a stately affair with white columns and a long blacktop driveway. The expansive property was beautiful, but impossible to protect with his limited manpower. There was at least a quarter mile between neighbors.

He stopped at the end of the tree-lined drive, unsure where to park. "You grew up here?" A new Jeep with two bright orange kayaks on top sat outside an oversized detached garage. "Is that Kara's car?"

"No. That's my mom's."

A moment later, Marissa's door closed behind her. She was halfway up the walk before he shifted into Park.

Marissa's arms stretched wide as an older version of herself launched off the porch and wrapped her in a rocking hug.

He ejected his key from the ignition and stretched onto his feet outside the cab.

The six-man sheriff's department in Shadow Point was already in over its head, and his team was working at capacity. There was no way he could properly protect a property this size. He moved slowly up the walk, thinking of how to keep the Lanes safe. Maybe his dad could invite himself over for a while. One trained man inside with the family was a smarter move than five wandering the property anyway.

He turned his phone in his palm and sent his father a text.

"Mom, this is Blake Garrett," Marissa said, drawing his attention back to the women on the walk. "He's the federal agent heading up the case."

The apparent note of pride in her voice stirred something loose in his chest. "Hello." He struggled to ignore the emotion and concentrate on making a good impression. After all, he was there to deliver the heinous details of a madman's actions, and ask this woman to trust him with her daughter's life. "It's nice to meet you, Mrs. Lane." He shook the woman's hand. "Kara's not here yet?"

Marissa's mom dragged her gaze back to Marissa's beat-up face. Her expression teetered between horror and confusion. "Not yet. She's on her way. Why?"

Blake did the numbers mentally. If Kara had been anywhere in town, and spoken to her mom before Marissa had, then Kara should've beaten them there. Even if she'd stopped somewhere along the way, she should have arrived by now. "When was the last time you spoke with her?"

Mrs. Lane shook her head. "She just texts. I'm sure she'll be here any minute."

He forced a tight smile, hoping to break the unbearable tension and get down to business. Kara was late and that was bad. "We're having trouble reaching her by phone."

"I'll send her a text. I'm sure she's gotten distracted by a rare bird or pack of Boy Scouts, or anything really. Kara's like that." Mrs. Lane took her time looking Blake over. Her worn blue jeans and white thermal shirt looked nearly as casual as her bare feet and sagging ponytail. Marissa had clearly been cut from this cloth. “You know, I’ve lived in Shadow Point all my life, even raised two daughters here, but I believe you’re the first Garrett to show up on my doorstep.”

He rested his hands on his hips, unreasonably pleased to know none of his brothers had been here before him. “Is that so?”

“I’ve heard a lot of interesting things about your family.”

Blake didn’t love the way she’d said *interesting*. “Nothing too bad, I hope.”

“Depends who’s telling the stories.”

Marissa blushed. “Mom.”

“Ah.” Blake had heard it all before. The Garretts were testosterone-driven cavemen, womanizers, married to the law and addicted to the chase. The last accusation wasn’t limited to bad guys. “We’re not so bad.”

The front door opened with a snap, and a man Blake’s father’s age stepped onto the porch. His no-nonsense stance and heavy frown screamed military. No wonder Marissa had been able to fight Nash off. This man seemed the sort to require combat training before starting public kindergarten. “Well, don’t just stand around in the open with a target on your backs,” he demanded.

Marissa jogged up the wide front steps and wrapped her arms around his middle. “Hi, Daddy.” She kissed his cheek with a relieved smile. His face went soft for a fleeting moment before turning sternly back to Blake.

"That lunatic's face is on every news station."

Marissa released him, and he gave her a closer look. "Good heavens." He skimmed a parental palm over her cheek, gently pushing the blond hair off her shoulder, revealing the evidence of Nash's fingers on her throat. "What the hell happened to you?"

"I told you yesterday. I was attacked. I fought him off," she said, flinging hair back over the marks on her neck. "Ran to the road and got a ride to the police station."

Her dad looked at her mom. "She got into a stranger's car after being attacked."

Getting into cars with strangers wasn't a move Blake personally recommended, but she was fleeing a crime scene. She needed help. "She's a fighter," Blake interjected with a ripple of misplaced pride.

"I know that," her father snapped. "Where were you while this was happening to my daughter?" He raised his hand to the bruising on her face.

"Louisville. I came as soon as I got the call from Sheriff Garrett. Thanks to Marissa, we were able to positively identify the man who did this. We put his name and face on the news hoping someone can help us find him."

Marissa motioned Blake to her side and gave the driveway a longing look, no doubt hoping for Kara's car to appear. "Come on," she said. "We can wait inside."

"That's what I said," her father grouched.

They were greeted by a soaring foyer with winding wooden stairs to the second floor. The floor plan was open. Walls were drenched in earth tones and family photos of the Lanes over the years. A fire roared in an exquisite stone fireplace at the head of their gathering room.

Blake took note of the expansive windows throughout and patio doors in both the dining and kitchen area. Too many access points. “Do you have a home security system, Mr. Lane?”

Marissa’s dad cast a look over his shoulder as they moved past the stairs toward the kitchen. “The wife and I have matching rifles and fifty years’ experience knocking dust off tin cans. Does that count?”

Everything about him said he’d hit more than tin cans. “It helps,” Blake admitted, “but a direct line to the authorities would be better. I’d like to station a man here until this blows over.”

Mr. Lane stopped moving where wide-planked wooden floors turned to mosaic tile. “I’ll accept help during the night shift. I can handle things during the day.”

That was reasonable, but unacceptable. His dad would have to bring a rocker and sit on the porch then. “I’d also like to see Kara stay with you for a few days,” Blake said.

“What about Marissa?” her father asked.

With enough men stationed here, Blake could probably keep her safe. He could take double shifts and bring additional people to protect the property. Hell, his cousin owned a private security firm, but something told Blake not to let her out of his sight. Whether it was professional instinct or plain personal interest, he couldn't say and didn't care. "I think she's safer with my team, sir."

Marissa squeezed between the men. "I smell coffee. Is there coffee?" She grabbed Blake's wrist and towed him to a granite-topped island. "Black?"

"Yes." He swung his attention to her mother who busily tapped her cell phone screen. "When did you get the last text from Kara?"

Marissa set a mug in front of him, then lined four more cups on the counter. She filled three to their rims and eagerly lifted one to her lips.

Her mom folded her arms, clearly uneasy. "Not long ago. Maybe forty minutes, but she was finishing a hike. Then, she needed to run home for some clean things to change into."

Marissa's shoulders collapsed. The coffee danced inside her mug from the slight trembles wracking her upper body.

Blake imagined folding her against his chest and telling her everything was going to be okay. Hell, if he could just put a hand over hers like he had in his truck, but she was flanked by her parents. A moment later, she leaned into her dad. "We were just at her house. She wasn't there."

Her mom paled. "Why were you at her house? Do you think something happened to her? What aren't you telling us?"

Blake ran his thumbs over the screen of his phone. "I'll check with Cole and see if she showed after we left, or if the neighbors remember seeing her before we got there."

He lifted his eyes to Marissa and her parents. "I'm truly sorry to be here under these circumstances. What does Kara drive and which direction would she have been coming? You said she'd planned to stop at her home before coming here?"

Marissa tapped her phone screen, presumably still trying to reach her sister. "She drives a Jeep like Mom and me. It's gunmetal gray. She bought it new last summer." She pressed the heel of one hand against her right eye. "She was hiking when I talked to her, too."

Her mother's jaw dropped. "You spoke to her? All I get are texts and little cartoon faces."

"I called her. She answered." Marissa set her phone on the counter. "I wish she'd just answer now."

Blake sent the make and model of Kara's car to his and West's teams. "Where was she hiking? We can contact gas stations between there and her home."

Marissa's face reddened. "I didn't ask."

Mrs. Lane let out a sharp breath and fixed Blake with a pointed stare. "She wouldn't be in the national park after what happened to Marissa, but there's no telling where she went. Now. Enough of this. Tell me what's going on and why my daughters are involved."

Mr. Lane crossed his arms and moved beside his wife.

Blake pushed his cup aside, shoring up the energy to lay it all out from the beginning. "It started for me about five years ago."

Forty-five minutes later, and seated around the living room with Marissa at his side, the story had been told, and the Lanes' questions had all been answered. Expect for the most important one. Where was Kara?

No one had seen her, and she hadn't answered her phone in two hours.

The realization that Kara wasn't coming arrived on the heels of a detailed description from Marissa about the last two days, including the strange luggage and ominous veil on Kara's porch.

Blake had let her take the lead on those events. They were hers to tell, personal in ways he wished they weren't. He'd filled in the larger aspects of the case and the role he'd played in it from the beginning.

Marissa pressed her hands to her face and stifled a small sob, the first she'd allowed today, despite all she'd seen. To Blake's surprise, she leaned against his side and set her head against his shoulder.

Blake wrapped an arm around her and turned his mouth toward her hair. "We'll find her, I promise." He inhaled the soft scent of her shampoo and imagined idly waking up to it every morning. The notion took him off guard. Blake hadn't had thoughts like that in a very long time. Reasonably so. Still, he liked the idea of knowing Marissa long after this case was closed. He tipped his cheek to her head in wonder.

Her mother's eyebrows rose. Her father's eyes narrowed.

Blake was as shocked as they were by the bond forming between him and Marissa, but she needed his strength at the moment and he wasn't going to let her go for a few judgmental looks. He'd fix the mess he created five years ago and bring Kara home safely to the Lanes.

He wasn't the sort of man who broke promises.

BLAKE'S PHONE BUZZED for the thirtieth time in as many minutes. He'd received nearly nonstop texts and emails as they'd told her parents about Nash Barclay. Until now, Blake had shared the information. This time, though, he excused himself to take the call.

Marissa followed him through the house and watched from the front window as he paced the porch.

Her mom and dad moved in on her like bookends, each winding one arm across her back. "Do you trust him?" her mother asked. "Can he do the things he says? Bring Kara home? Catch this maniac?"

"Yes." Marissa felt the truth of the words in her core. "We don't know where Kara is yet, but if we find out she's in trouble, then I trust Blake to bring her home."

Her dad harrumphed. "I think you'd be better off staying with us while he goes back into the field. You're our top priority. Let the sonofagun who's doing this be his. With you here, Agent Garrett can actively hunt this man."

Marissa's muscles bunched, the way they always seemed to at the thought of leaving Blake's side. Nash was probably watching them, even now, and staying together was smart. Besides, staying at her parents' home could put them in danger. She eased the sheer curtain aside with her fingertips and attempted to decode his muffled voice through the glass.

"He's too distracted," her dad continued. "Troubled. That's no way to lead an investigation."

Marissa gave her dad a sad smile. "You heard him. He blames himself for what happened to those women."

"And you," he said, frustration creeping into his voice. "This is happening to you, too, and your sister. This isn't about some strangers. My daughters are involved now." His voice cracked, and he turned away with a curse.

"I know," Marissa said. In fact, Nash was only after Kara because Marissa had gotten away. That was on her.

The front door opened, and Blake poked his head inside. "Time to go. They've got a lead on the truck."

Marissa drifted away from her parents. "And Kara?"

He shook his head infinitesimally. "Not yet."

"Don't go," her mom pleaded.

Marissa went back to squeeze her mom. "I'm going to be okay, and you can reach me anytime you want at the number I called from earlier, okay? I won't be alone. I've got Blake and his team, plus the sheriff and his deputies looking out for me."

Frustration burned in her dad's cheeks. His eyes

were glossed with fear. "Anything happens to her, Garrett, and I'm holding you responsible."

Blake moved into their home, standing close and strong at Marissa's back. "Sir, you can rest assured that I will protect both your daughters at any cost."

Her dad's chin wobbled. "Do that."

Blake's hand was on Marissa's waist, turning her toward the waiting truck. "Time to go."

She took one last look at her parents, then let Blake lead her away. Frightened as she was for whatever lay ahead, Marissa was certain she could face it with Blake. She was also thankful for how shockingly natural it felt to lean on him for support. Yesterday, he'd been a stranger, and today he was her friend. More than that. Was there even a word to explain all Blake had become for her? The way he willingly shouldered her burdens? No one had ever done that, and Blake wasn't only strong when she was weak, but he was intuitive and kind. She trusted him to get her through whatever came next, and with a little luck that wouldn't involve any more bodies of Nash's victims.

Her baby sister's included.

Chapter Seven

Blake shifted into Drive and inched toward the road, discouraged by the Lanes' vast amount of land and lack of nosy neighbors. Hopefully his dad wouldn't be much longer. He'd responded affirmatively to Blake's text request for him to drop in on Marissa's family. Leaving the Lanes alone wasn't Blake's first choice, but he was needed at the station, and his dad was a solid stand-in. The town's former sheriff had training, experience and an innate compulsion to protect and serve. Exactly what the Lanes needed in a bodyguard.

Marissa turned weary eyes on Blake. "What happened? Where are we going?"

"Back to the sheriff's department. Cole says there's been an onslaught of sightings since the media picked up Nash's story, and they need help taking statements. He's pulled in a handful of volunteers meeting with folks in person, and West has Mom's quilting club manning the phones."

Marissa kneaded her hands on her lap. "You didn't get bad news about Kara then."

"No." Blake paused at the end of the Lanes' driveway. "I wouldn't keep news about your sister from you."

The street was quiet, no traffic, no vehicles parked curbside. That was all good, but a jogger rounding the distant bend set off his internal radar. Blake added pressure to the brake, stopping to monitor the man. "You recognize him?"

"No." Marissa leaned forward. "He's too far away."

"All right." Blake freed his side arm and rested it against his thigh, then eased onto the road, moving them slowly in the man's direction.

His face was hidden beneath the shadow of a high-end hoodie. The brand symbol was printed in reflective silver across his chest. He had the posture of a runner. His strides were steady and evenly paced. He didn't appear to be out of breath or excessively distracted. No indication of unusual interest in the surrounding properties, specifically the Lanes'.

He looked into the truck's window and lifted a hand in greeting as they crawled past.

Marissa relaxed against the seatback. "It's not him."

Blake slid his trigger finger out of position, curling it back with the others. "Good." He reholstered his sidearm and tried to ignore the pinch of disappointment. If the jogger had been Nash, Blake could've watched his expression as he made him pay for everything he'd done.

Marissa twisted in her seat belt, straining to look

through the back window. "Someone's turning onto my parents' drive." Panic raised her soft voice to a new octave. "I don't know that truck."

The small black Ford disappeared from sight in Blake's rearview as it motored toward the Lane home. "I asked my dad to stop by. See if there's anything he can do to curb their fears."

"You sent him to guard them?" Her voice quivered on the last word.

"Yeah." Blake took the next left and stole a look at her bruised face. His fingers tightened on the wheel. "It's precautionary. Nothing more."

Her shoulders relaxed by a small measure.

"How is it that you're so calm?" he asked. Most people he protected had at least one outburst by now, and their threats weren't always as immediate. He expected tears. Rage. Something. People in Marissa's position usually found someone in law enforcement to blame for their circumstance or a reason to complain about the way Blake handled the case. Instead, she'd been instrumental in every step of progress they'd made. "You were smart to think of the lake town." His stomach rolled at the memory of all those women being pulled ashore. "You did a mighty thing."

She pursed her lips and looked away, watching the view outside her window. "Lucky guess."

"And the calm front you're wearing?"

"A disguise." The inflection in her voice suggested she wasn't sure. "Maybe mind over matter.

I don't know. I've always been pretty good at compartmentalizing in times of strife or challenge. I break big obstacles into smaller, more manageable tasks, then I handle the pieces one at a time. I use the same method to reach personal goals. It's how I got through college while working full-time, and pretty much how I learn to do anything. Horseback riding. Rock climbing. Nothing comes easily for me. I'm just a natural-born hardhead, and I guess I'm applying those strategies now. I hadn't really thought about it."

"Well, it's working."

"It's how I got away," she said, taking a look in his direction. "Now that you've mentioned it, focusing on the small picture is probably the only reason I'm not in the bathtub back at the hotel wound into the fetal position." She turned back to her window. "Besides, panic has never helped anyone accomplish anything, and Kara needs me to stay focused. I'll have a proper breakdown later. Privately."

Emotion welled in Blake's chest. He didn't like the thought of her alone and upset in a bathtub or anywhere else. "You can talk to me," he said, "if you want." He'd like that. Marissa was strong, maybe even the kind of woman who could handle life with someone like him, a man who spent his life in a perpetual state of danger. Most women either couldn't or wouldn't, but he suspected Marissa was fully capable of anything.

Truth be told, the Garrett boys' reputation for

being a matched set of untamable playboys was deeply ironic. Even if they wanted to settle down, how would they find someone willing to endure life with a lawman? It was easier not to think past the third date than to haplessly search for someone who didn't exist.

"What?" Marissa asked.

Blake started. "What?"

"You shook your head. Was that because of what I said?"

"No."

Her gaze warmed the side of Blake's face.

He waited. Apparently, she had something to ask, and he knew firsthand how difficult it could be to put some things into words. Considering all that Marissa was going through, she deserved to take as long as she wanted. Personally, he found it easier to keep things to himself, speaking only when necessary and never longer than he had to. The practice had served him well as an agent. When he had something to say, his team knew it was worth hearing, and they listened.

Marissa lifted and dropped her hands against her thighs. "My dad thinks I should have stayed with him."

Blake's gaze jumped to hers, then back to the road. The uncertainty in her tone was a blow to his chest. Did she think her dad could keep her safer? Was that possible? Or was it something else? Maybe she wanted a break from Blake's constant presence and was too polite or overwhelmed to say so. He'd been enjoying their dynamic, but he hadn't considered how she might feel. Stifled. Smothered. Unhappy. He slowed the truck. "Nash is looking for you, so your presence will add to their risk. I won't stop you from going back, but I'm staying with you wherever you are." He could keep watch from outside if she needed a break from him.

Her blue eyes widened. "No. I want to stay with you."

His grip on the wheel loosened. "Okay." He turned back to the road with relief and nonsensical pride. "Then why'd you bring that up?"

She bit into the thick of her bottom lip and furrowed her brows. "My dad thinks I'm keeping you from playing a more active role in Nash's pursuit, and I think you should focus on the case and stop worrying so much about me. I don't want to be the thing that holds you back."

The sincerity in her eyes and voice sliced straight through him. He pulled the truck over and twisted on the seat to face her. "Your dad is wrong."

She wet her lips and waited, for what he wasn't sure, but the words from his head were piling on his tongue faster than he could sort them. "We're sticking together," he said. "If you're not with me, then I'll be worrying about you, and that's no good. My men can handle the field while I take point. We're doing it this way because it's the only way that makes sense, not because you're holding me back."

His shoulders sagged as he worked the truth over in his mind. He'd taken himself out of play on the most important case of his career. For years, he'd dreamed of tearing into Nash with his bare hands, and now he'd relegated himself to a desk. He'd done it so Marissa would be safer and feel less afraid.

Blake turned stiffly back to the wheel and angled the truck onto the road. The realization was a load of bricks dumped over him. Marissa's dad couldn't have been more wrong. Her presence wasn't compromising Blake's investigation. Meeting her had compromised *him.*

MARISSA GAWKED AT the line of people extended along the front of the sheriff's department.

Blake parked on the sidewalk outside the crowded lot. He circled the truck and opened the passenger door for her.

"Are these all volunteers?" she asked.

"Sadly, no." He offered her a hand out of the vehicle, then closed the door behind her. "Those are all witnesses." The sour look on his face said he didn't believe half of them had witnessed anything other than the morning newscast. "Excuse us," he said, escorting Marissa inside.

As promised, a gaggle of women her mom's age filled the seats at a row of newly erected tables near the far wall. Old-fashioned telephones with landlines had been set up in front of each seat like a telethon. "Is that your mom's quilting crew?"

He gave the group a peculiar look. "None other."

A pair of Shadow Point deputies conducted interviews at their desks, while an agent with a clipboard spoke to the next person in line.

Marissa looked to Blake. “Are all these people good news or bad?” It seemed the verdict could go either way.

Blake rubbed the stubble on his chin. “A little of both, I guess. Good news is that we know the newscast made an impression. Bad news is we have to sift through all the chaff to find the wheat, if there is any, and then hope we aren’t too late to act on the intel.”

Marissa’s muscles tightened and her throat clogged at the implication. “I see.”

Blake’s hand found the small of her waist. He tipped his head downward, forming a private conversation space. “Hey. I didn’t mean *too late for Kara*. I meant that if it takes us too long to learn Nash’s whereabouts, and he moves on, then even the good information is still useless, and the efforts here are in vain. Timing’s everything in cases like these.”

Marissa smoothed sweat-slicked palms against her jeans. “Where should I sit?”

“Break room?” He lifted his brows in question.

Marissa cocked her head back. “If the local quilting crew can take calls, I can talk to the people in line. I know what he looks like. I’ll know if someone really saw him.”

Blake hunched lower into their private cocoon. His fingers relaxed, settling into the curve of her hip. “Listening to false reports can be infuriating. You don't have to put yourself through any unnecessary ordeals. You've already done more than anyone expected." His voice was low and careful, evidently meant to protect her from potential trauma.

She formed her most pleading expression and matched his cautious tone. "You just said timing is everything, and I can help you get through this line of people waiting to be heard." Blake had made it clear that his job was to protect her, but her job was to protect Kara, and if listening to some cuckoo stories was the fastest way to get the facts, then that's what she would do.

Blake didn't answer. Instead, the two of them locked determined gazes.

"Hello." A woman's voice sounded nearby, and a shadow fell over them.

Blake turned his eyes on her without relaxing his stance. Mixed emotions flitted over his handsome face before he straightened. "Mama."

The woman's attention darted from her son's face to his hand on Marissa. "This must be Miss Lane." She squinted at the marks on Marissa's face before settling into a small smile. "I've heard a lot about you today. You're in good hands, now. I promise."

Blake dropped his hand away and rolled his shoulders back.

Marissa offered his mother a hand to shake. "It's nice to meet you. I hope Blake's said nice things."

"I haven't heard a thing from Blake." She gave

him a curious look as she took Marissa's hand. "I've spoken to West, Cole and their father, but not Blake."

Marissa ignored the senseless tug of disappointment. Of course Blake hadn't rushed to call his mom and tell her all about her. This was business for him. Marissa, on the other hand, had too many emotions and not enough sleep.

Blake's chest expanded and fell in a silent sigh. "I've meant to call. I've had my hands full."

"Yes, I saw." She smiled warmly at Marissa. "Is there anything I can do to make you more comfortable?"

"I'm fine." She pushed her hand into her pocket hoping it wasn't too clammy during the shake. "I was just asking Blake where I should sit to help with witness statements."

A mix of surprise and pleasure flitted over his mother's face. She turned mischievous eyes on Blake. "Why don't I show her to the community bulletin table? No one's using that space." She started toward the far wall and motioned them to follow.

They stopped at a four-foot folding table. Blake stacked the piles of community event flyers in a heap and moved them to the center. He released a sharp whistle, and Marissa flinched.

A passing deputy stopped to look their way.

"Can I get two chairs over here?" Blake asked.

"Yes, sir."

Blake rested his fists on the wobbly structure.

"This will work. I'll take one end and review reports while you talk to witnesses on the other."

Blake's mom shot him a look and returned to the table lined with middle-aged women and ringing phones.

"Great." Marissa fought a wave of nausea. She even needed a protective detail inside the sheriff's department. She was in so much danger that she was being escorted around town by a federal agent. Her breaths came short and hot.

"Marissa?" The warmth of Blake's body was back in her space. Scents of his cologne and aftershave were everywhere. "Are you okay? Remember. You don't have to do this."

She swallowed the lump of fear in her throat and nodded.

Did he really think someone might try to hurt her at the sheriff's department? Was Nash Barclay that bold?

The deputy arrived with a pair of folding chairs. "Anything else?" His gaze lingered on Marissa's swollen cheek.

She swept the length of her hair over one shoulder and let the thick strands form a veil over the marks on her fast-heating face.

"No." Blake took the chairs and opened them, setting one at each end of the table.

Her knees buckled easily as she fell onto the seat. Blake watched with a heartbreaking expression. She would've asked what he was thinking, but where would that get her? Blake wasn't exactly a sharer. If he wanted her to know something, he'd volunteer it. Besides, it wasn't as if that look had anything to do with her, and if it wasn't about her or her sister, then it wasn't any of Marissa's business.

She pulled her attention to the line at the door. "I'm going to collect my first witness." She had plenty of work to do and all night to speculate about the cause of Blake's troubled face.

"I'll be here if you need me."

If there was ever a Blake Garrett action figure, that would be the tagline.

Marissa faltered only steps from the double glass doors. Her heart rate kicked up, and she felt the chill of fear roll down her spine. "Blake."

Amidst the white noise of traffic and soft rumble of the crowd, another sound trickled into her ears. "Blake?"

He was at her side in an instant. "What is it? What's wrong?" His hands were on her hips, his cautious blue eyes weighted with worry.

"I hear his song." She raised a finger to her lips. "Listen."

Blake jerked his head around to face the lot. "Stay here." His eyes widened, and he barreled outside with one hand on his sidearm.

Marissa clutched her chest and crept closer to the open door, torn between wanting the song to be in her imagination and not wanting to be crazy.

Silence fell over the witnesses as they moved

against the building in an awkward wave, nudging one another and pointing as Blake rounded each car and surveyed their faces.

West and a pair of agents strode into the lot where Blake stood.

Nash's creepy chapel song blared from the pocket of a black hoodie.

A sheen of sweat formed on Marissa's brow. Nash's hot breath blew fresh on her face, as real and sickening as the day they'd met. She rubbed her heated cheeks and shuffled through the doors, desperate to know what would happen next.

Blake snaked an arm out and spun the person around.

The hood fell back to reveal a homeless-looking woman with ratty blond hair. "I saw him," she said with a grin.

Blake yanked an old CD player from the hoodie and jammed his finger against the power button, ending the awful tune.

Marissa's shoulders sagged with release.

"He gave me a coat, money, music and a sandwich," the woman said. "All I had to do was stand here until I got the chance to tell you." Her wide toothless smile sent tremors over Marissa's frame.

Didn't the woman understand her benefactor was a cold-blooded killer? Didn't she know? He could have hurt her. Drowned her.

A fat tear rolled over Marissa's cheek and she sucked in another ragged breath before turning back for the station. Surrounded by law enforcement, and Nash had still been right outside the glass double doors.

Marissa wasn't safe anywhere.

Chapter Eight

It was after four before Blake had a chance to check in with West again. He knocked on his brother's open office door and wedged himself in the threshold. "A line of witnesses around the building and no one saw anything."

West looked up from his file. "You mean no one except the nice homeless woman."

Blake rolled his back against the jamb and rested his head on the cool metal. "The one who spoke of Nash as if he were the Messiah, bringing her a warm jacket, music from her heyday and money?"

"That's the one."

Blake blew out a long breath. "What'd you do with her anyway?" The woman had been gone when he and two of his team members finished scouting the area for signs of Nash nearby.

"I took her statement then drove her to a shelter where she could get a hot meal and a warm bed for the night. I put the sweatshirt into evidence with the CD player and gave her a replacement with a little cash for her trouble."

"Great."

West hunched over his desk as Blake stepped into the hall. "Where are you going?"

"To find Marissa. I'm going to see if I can get her out of here. Get some food. Get some sleep." He'd tried to coax her away an hour ago, but she'd insisted on staying until the last witness was heard.

As if her day hadn't been bad enough, there wasn't any news about her sister, and Kara was still unaccounted for.

Blake returned to their table and slid copies of the most promising witness accounts into a manila envelope for later.

Marissa's head was on the desk, one cheek cradled in the crook of an arm. Her free hand dangled at her side. It would've been a peaceful scene, if the marks of a lunatic weren't displayed across her visible cheek and throat. She'd done her best to hide the evidence behind her hair as "witnesses" made their statements, but the fight was now lost to exhaustion.

"Ready?" he asked. Blake moved to her side, gut and jaw clenched as he imagined the terror and confusion when Nash attacked her. He'd come so close to losing her that day. Except that wasn't true. He hadn't known her then. So, how did a woman he'd met less than forty-eight hours ago feel like she'd been a part of his life forever?

"Marissa." He squatted beside her chair and used his most soothing voice so as not to startle her. "Marissa." His fingers ached to reach for hers, to twine them with his, or maybe just pull her into his arms.

Blake let his lids fall shut for a quick internal curse. He could *admire* her without *touching* her. He needed to get thoughts of the latter out of his head.

He scanned the room for prying eyes and found plenty. His brother, West, was among the spectators. Two members of his team turned away when they were caught staring, but West crossed his arms and rocked back on his heels, a distinct look of interest on his brow. Blake didn't like it. What did it mean? Surely it wasn't romantic interest in Marissa. He felt his scowl deepen. "Marissa," he repeated, slightly louder this time. "Hey." He lifted her hand in his and met West's gaze once more.

She stirred at his touch. "Hi." She blinked unwilling eyes. "I fell asleep." Her small hand turned against his, locking their palms.

A shock of victory blazed through him at her small acceptance. "Time to go back to the hotel. Can you walk or would you like me to carry you?" he teased, feeling much too light for the day they'd had.

"Both?" She squinted up at him with a lazy smile.

He tamped down a broad grin and stole another look around the room before leaning closer. "I wouldn't mind carrying you, but I think that might get some rumors started."

Across the room, West headed into his office with a smirk.

The haze of sleep fell from Marissa's face, and her smile went flat. "Sorry." She freed her hand from his and used it to straighten her hair and shirt, then to wipe the corners of her mouth and eyes.

Blake returned to his side of the desk, unsure what had happened in the moment between her dreamy hello and near-instant recoil. Had she initially mistaken him for someone else? Had he offended her by being overly playful on what must be the worst day of her life? He made a trip around the room while she got her bearings and gathered her things.

Once his team had their orders, he leaned against the doorjamb of West's office and waited for his brother to take notice. "We're headed out."

West dropped his pen onto the desk and stretched. "Sounds good. If I get anything substantial, I'll route it in your direction. You need anything else?"

Blake relaxed against the cool metal frame. "Besides Nash Barclay in cuffs or a pine box? Not really." And preferably neither. Nash didn't deserve the life sentence he'd get for his crimes. Hell, he didn't deserve a pine box. What he needed was to be kicked into the lake and assigned the same fate he'd given those poor women.

West interlocked his fingers behind his head, elbows pointed skyward. "We're going to get that done, brother."

Marissa appeared in Blake's periphery, emerging from the restroom and looking somewhat revived. Her hair was split into low pigtails and arranged over her shoulders, probably to mask the marks on her neck. Her cheeks were pale with exhaustion and a swath of loose hair fell over her bruised cheek. "Are we still leaving?" she asked, stopping inches from his side.

"Yeah." Blake shook the vengeful thoughts from his mind and refocused on the beauty before him. She needed words of hope and comfort, not a list of ways he wanted to see Nash punished. "West and I were just wrapping things up."

West rocked out of his office chair and moseyed to his filing cabinet. "I was just telling Blake that I'd pass along any information that seems solid. You guys both look like you could use some sleep." He opened the bottom drawer and tossed a duffel bag at Blake. "I got you something."

Blake pulled the zipper back. "What is it?"

"I brought you a couple changes of clothes and stopped for some basic bathroom stuff. I thought you could use it."

Blake had left Louisville the moment West called yesterday morning. He'd torn out of town with one thing on his mind, and it wasn't a change of clothes or toothpaste. "Thanks, man." Now, he wouldn't have to make a stop at the store for those things. He could stay on task.

Marissa fidgeted beside him, eyes fixed on West. "No word on my sister?"

West's gaze swept to Blake, then back to Marissa. He shifted his stance and seemed to weigh his words. "Nothing yet, but remember it's only been a few hours, and if not for the picture Blake found, a four-hour absence wouldn't be cause for concern. We're on guard because of it, but the truth is that photo wasn't taken today. Based on background structures and foliage, I'd say it's at least three months old and shot at a crowded event. The image could've been pulled off the internet. It could be nothing more than psychological warfare aimed at you or Blake. We just don't know."

Tears sprang to her eyes. "Of course."

Blake curved a protective arm over her shoulders and narrowed his eyes on West.

He shrugged. "What?"

Blake wasn't the only one in the family who was better off keeping his mouth shut. Psychological warfare? Way to make an already terrifying situation worse. He shook his head at West, and ushered Marissa toward the front door. Everything West had said was true, but Marissa wasn't a lawman. She hadn't signed up to live in this world, and she didn't need to hear all the ways a man like Nash Barclay was likely to taunt her.

He fought an unstoppable yawn. West was right about something else, too. Blake and Marissa both needed some sleep.

It was only a matter of time before Nash struck again.

THE DRIVE UP the mountain was beautiful. Blake took it slowly enough for Marissa to enjoy the gently swaying trees and familiar bends in the country road. The sky was a glorious mix of apricot and amber, bringing harmony and peace to her cluttered mind. She dragged a fingertip over the passenger window. "I appreciated what your brother said back there."

Blake slid his eyes her way, then back to the road. "Yeah?"

"It probably looked like he upset me, but that wasn't it. That was the first time anyone has reminded me that there are other alternatives to this for Kara. There's still a chance she's out there doing something completely normal with plans to go to Mom and Dad's place as soon as she finishes." Marissa just wished she could think of a few reasonable possibilities. "She's carefree to the extreme. Sometimes a little flighty, but she's smart. Just young. I said there was a fugitive in town. She wanted to hike, so she probably left town to do it. She's like that, and I like thinking that she'll still turn up today, happy and unscathed."

Wisps of feathery gray clouds flitted into view as the sun dipped lower on the horizon. Barely after five o'clock and the world was already tinted by night's approach. Whatever Kara was doing, she'd have to wrap it up soon. There was barely an hour of sunlight left.

Blake slowed for the turn at the resort entrance. "I used to ski here. The slopes are nice." He cruised between large stone columns marking the final leg to their room on the hill. "Do you ski?"

She made a show of rolling her eyes and gave a small smile. "Of course. I'm a little impressed that you do."

"I'm not any good."

Marissa doubted that. "Did you know there are some beautiful caves on this side of the mountain?

I've actually spent a lot of time here spelunking. I've gotten some amazing photos for the effort."

"What kind of caves? Bear caves? Bats?"

"Probably both, but I didn't run into either. The caves' mouths are fairly well hidden by natural camouflage, jagged rocks, clay, that sort of thing. If you ever have time, you should see for yourself. The moss is gorgeous near the mouths, and the ecosystems inside are fascinating."

He squinted through the windshield, presumably trying to see a hidden cave from their position on the road. A moment later he passed the hotel without slowing.

"What are you doing?" Marissa twisted for a view of the lodge sign disappearing behind them.

"I'm buying you dinner." He pulled off at an old diner just outside of town. "Ever been here?"

"Not since I was young. We came here for ice cream after softball games."

Blake loped around the front of the truck and opened her door. "Us, too. Baseball, then peewee football. I think we were here every Friday night for a decade."

Marissa smiled, filled with nostalgia and renewed energy. "I bet we were here at the same time once or twice. I would've been in middle school during your last few visits." She liked knowing Blake was from her hometown. There was a certain camaraderie in loving the same beautiful place and sharing childhood memories of the same locations.

He escorted her inside with a hand on her back and chose a table against the far wall.

The place hadn't changed. It still smelled of stale black coffee and apple pie. Same brown tile flooring and cracked orange-vinyl seats. A bar ran the length of the narrow rectangular space.

Blake's gaze made a continuous circuit through the parking lot and across the front door as the waitress took their order. Chili and coffee for him, chicken noodle soup and water for Marissa. Though she doubted she could eat anything until she knew Kara was safe.

She checked the large oval clock above the counter. "Kara should be home anytime. There's nowhere to jog or hike after dark."

Blake shifted forward in his seat, sliding his arms over the table's cool surface, and clutched her trembling hands in his steady ones. He stroked the warm pads of his thumbs over her skin. "We'll find her." There was fierce promise in his eyes.

Marissa's worried mind began to settle, but her body was winding up once more.

Too soon, the waitress ferried drinks and meals to the table, effectively breaking Blake's spell. He pulled his hands back to his sides and dug into the chili with gusto.

Marissa rubbed her hands together beneath the table, wishing she could trade the noodle soup for more of Blake's confident touch.

He tapped a packet of crackers against the table, seemingly unaffected by the moment they'd shared.

"When we met, you asked me if I'd always wanted to be an agent. Have you always wanted to be a nature photographer?"

She dipped a spoon into her soup, dunking a thick homemade noodle and releasing rich buttery scents into the air. "No. I've always wanted to be a mom." Her cheeks heated immediately, wishing she hadn't been so transparent with a man who would probably never have the time or desire for a family of his own. Not that her life plans would matter to him. She stuffed the spoon into her mouth before she said anything else she'd regret.

"That so?" His cheek kicked up. "Would you just put the baby in one of those backpacks and hit the trails?"

"Probably." Marissa sighed. Leave it to him to make her feel completely normal about making family plans when she hadn't been on a date in over a year. "That's pretty much what my mom did with us. She never stopped moving, and neither have we. What about you? Did you always want to be a fed? You didn't answer me before."

Blake gave Marissa a long, careful look. "Nah. I wanted to be a judge. They have the real power to make things right. I can haul criminals in all day, but it's the judges who make the big decisions from there."

"But judges can't do any good if people like you don't risk everything to bring the bad guys in." She tipped her head, trying to understand how someone went from wanting a seat behind a bench to chasing murderers. "What happened?"

He shot a guilty glance her way. "I went as far as finishing law school before the allure of the badge pulled me in."

"Wow. That's a powerful pull."

"You have no idea."

She imagined doing all the work it must've taken to complete law school, only to drop it all and go another way. Maybe protect and serve really was in the Garrett DNA.

"Dumb, right? I gave up a comfortable future for half the pay and ten times the personal injury."

Marissa leveled him with her most sincere stare. "No. I think you're exactly where you're supposed to be, doing exactly what you were called to do. You can't put a price on that."

His lips parted and his brows raised. "You have no idea what that means coming from you."

She dipped her spoon into the steamy broth and smiled, enjoying the swell in her chest. Federal Agent Blake Garrett was nothing like any man she'd ever met. He had brains and brawn, as well as a little more of her heart every time they spoke.

MARISSA EXCUSED HERSELF to the ladies' room, and Blake angled in his seat, attempting to keep an eye on both the front door and rear hallway. Two bites of chili later, he gave up and headed for the ladies' room.

“Oh!” She started at the sight of him in the narrow hallway.

“Sorry.” He dipped his head forward to rub the back of his neck. “I wasn’t sure if there was a rear entrance, so I thought I should keep watch by the door.”

Marissa looked strangely refreshed. She’d touched up her lip gloss and the baby hairs near her temple were speckled with tiny droplets of water.

She tucked a long blond strand behind one ear and smiled shyly. “I splashed some water on my face.” Her cheeks grew ruddy with the admission. “I looked awful.”

Blake doubted that Marissa had ever looked awful in her life. He watched with rapt attention as a small drop followed the curve of her jaw and traveled the length of her slender neck. Whatever she’d said next was lost to the thrumming in his chest. Blake drank her in with greedy eyes, from the flush of her skin to the gentle sway of her back. Marissa was breathtaking.

She moved slowly forward in the cramped space, stopping only when the toes of her shoes bumped his. “Please quit looking at me like I’m going to break.”

“I don’t think you’re going to break.” He raised his hand carefully, never taking his eyes off hers, allowing her every opportunity to back away like she had at the station when she woke. He was tired of fighting the urge to be closer to her, and she needed to know what she was doing to him. Her rejection would set him straight. It would put these ridiculous feelings to rest so he could start thinking of ways to keep her safe instead of ways to keep her near.

Her lids fell shut as the backs of his fingertips reached her cheek. He stroked the tender curve of her jaw before cupping it in both his palms.

The ache in his belly grew as he struggled to understand this thing that had taken hold of him from the moment she'd walked into his life.

Her lips parted on an intake of breath, and he strained against the need to taste them. He fought the crackling electricity coursing over his skin from hers, and he forced himself to think of the *right* thing. *For Marissa.*

"Blake." Her eyes eased open. Were they heavy with desire? Or was he merely hoping?

She lifted her hands to his chest, sliding them gently upward to his shoulders.

The buzz of his phone nearly killed him.

She dropped her forehead against his chest and exhaled a gush of warm breath. "Sorry."

"No." Blake glared at the blasted phone, his heart beating like horses' hooves against his ribs. "Do not be sorry." He lifted a finger as he studied the phone's small screen, then raised apologetic eyes to hers. "The coroner has preliminary findings."

"Okay." She inhaled deeply and squared her shoulders. "Let's go."

THE TRIP TO the coroner's office was quiet. He couldn't say where Marissa's thoughts were, but his were back at the restaurant with her hands winding over his shoulders.

"Garrett." An elderly man in a white lab coat greeted him at the front desk. "Your dad and I used to do this." He motioned between them.

Blake tried to smile, but failed. What he needed now were facts. Niceties could come later when he knew all there was to know about Nash's victims. "What do you have?"

"We've confirmed the identities of five of the six victims." He handed Blake a file folder. "I've put copies of all our preliminary data in there for you."

Blake scanned the pages. Four women were the victims whose families Blake had gotten to know in the course of his investigation. West had correctly identified the fifth victim as a recently missing jogger at the county line. "What about the woman who'd been down there longest?"

"That will take a while longer. She was in..." the man cast his gaze to Marissa before reaffixing it to Blake, "worse shape."

Blake flipped between the listed causes of death. "The victims were all drowned."

"Yes, that's correct."

Ice slid through Blake's veins. He'd wrongly assumed that Nash had killed the women elsewhere and dragged them to their watery graves afterward. He winced at the memory of scuba weights near the tree where Nash and Marissa had fought. Nash would have drowned Marissa in the lake and dressed her there, along the bank or underwater. So, the veil left on her bed was strictly meant to antagonize her after she'd gotten away. Just like the suitcases left on her sister's porch. Nash wanted to keep her afraid. Break her focus. Make her easier prey.

A sudden cacophony blasted outside the building. Marissa jumped at Blake's side, curling against him for safety.

"It's my truck alarm." He smoothed a palm down the length of her hair and back before peeling her away. He pointed at the man. "Take her into your office and lock the door."

Blake eased into the dark lot, gun drawn. The night was clear, and his truck undamaged, but a large white envelope was seated on his windshield. The sight of it turned Blake's stomach. Five small words were formed in soaking red ink.

A gift for the bride.

Chapter Nine

Blake's team and West's deputies filled the small sitting room at the hotel. The contents of the mysterious envelope were spread throughout the room, some on the small table, others pinned to a corkboard borrowed from the sheriff's department. The rest moved hand to hand through the room for inspection.

Together the stack of glossy surveillance photos was a quarter-inch thick, and Marissa was centered in each frame.

West sat on the edge of the sleeper sofa, elbows pressed against his knees. "He left them on your windshield?"

"Yep." Blake paced the patterned commercial carpeting, struggling for focus, the dangerous heat of vengeance roiling in his gut. "Set off my truck's alarm to make sure I knew he was there."

Marissa sat with West on the sofa, feet tucked beneath her. "They're just like the photo that someone took of Kara."

Blake ground his teeth. "Not someone. Nash." He

swore before turning back to his brother. "He's practically following me around and I can't find him."

West kneaded his hands where they hung between his knees. "At least tell me there were surveillance cameras where you parked."

Blake stopped to glare. The fire in his belly was nearly painful. "He looked right into the camera while he made the delivery."

"So it's on tape," West said. "That's good."

Blake leaned against the wall and tipped forward at the waist. He'd spent years thinking he was after an unhinged psychopath, but that wasn't who Nash was. The dresses. The underwater chapel. Months of dedicated stalking. Blake had him all wrong. Nash was a sociopath. Cold and calculating. Biding his time. Planning his kills. Probably enjoying the hunt as much as the attack.

"I found something else after you left the station," West said. "I pulled the missing person report on the woman abducted earlier this month. It struck me as inconsistent that he'd taken months between the other kills, then after five years off, he made two back-to-back attacks." He danced his thumbs over the screen of his phone.

Blake's cell phone buzzed on the table. He flipped it around to face him and typed in the access code.

It was a photo of the last woman to be pulled from the lake. She looked like Marissa. Marissa had said so herself.

Marissa peered at West's phone and made a strange gurgling sound. "I think I'm going to be sick."

In the photo, the woman was wearing the same fitted running gear Marissa had worn the morning of her attack.

Blake swallowed a mouthful of bile. Nash had mistaken her for Marissa. "He'd been expecting Marissa on that towpath."

West nodded. "I think so. The fitness app on Marissa's phone showed a pattern of morning trips to that park. Typically, Tuesday mornings, the same day of the week that this woman went missing."

Marissa's face paled impossibly further. "Sometimes, I skip my morning jog to meet Kara for breakfast. It's kind of our thing. Very impromptu. I'm always busy, and she slows me down with an unexpected invitation. I never say no." Until today. A tear rolled onto her cheek and she quickly swiped it away. "That woman is dead because of me?"

"No." Blake and West growled the answer.

Marissa scoffed. "He came for me. I wasn't there, and this poor woman has my taste in clothes." A painful wedge formed in her throat. "She was just living her life."

West angled on the couch to face her. "So were you. You didn't know you were being watched. How could you? No one knew."

The truth was another hot poker to Blake's gut. He should've known. He'd become lax this year. Assuming Nash was either dead or out of the country after such a long hiatus. He'd slowly stopped wasting federal time and money chasing vapor.

Maybe that was why Nash got back into the game.

Could he have known that Blake had moved on? Would Nash start killing again to regain Blake's attention?

Had he been watching Blake all this time?

MARISSA LEANED ON her forearms, trying to remain calm. Her heart sprinted and her chest heaved, desperate for more air than her lungs could find. She concentrated on breathing. Slow and steady. *This is what Nash wants*, she chided internally. *He wants you in an emotional frenzy.* Hadn't West said as much at the station? *Psychological warfare.*

Well, it was working.

The jogger had been murdered because of her. Her sister had possibly been abducted because of her.

It had to stop. "Use me as bait."

The men fell silent. She hadn't kept up with their conversation, but their voices were suddenly still.

She released an uneasy breath and levered herself upright. "Nash wants me, so let him have me."

Blake's eyes bulged briefly before narrowing into slits. "Absolutely not."

West leaned slightly forward, catching her eye. "It's a noble thought, but we aren't in the business of putting people in danger."

"Or giving animals like Nash Barclay exactly what they want," Blake barked.

Marissa pushed onto shaky legs and moved toward him. "So, don't give him what he wants." She turned to West. "Protect me." That covered both their arguments. "Use me to save my sister."

West groaned. "We don't know if he—"

She waved her hand to stop him. "Then use me to save the next lady." She turned back to Blake's glaring eyes. "There will always be a next victim unless you stop him."

"No."

"Blake."

"I said no." His words sliced through her.

She wouldn't win this battle. "Then there must be another way," she pleaded. "So, what is it? Because it's certainly not to sit in this room and wait for his next move. His next move could be murder." She folded her arms, hoping to look resolute and hating the hint of whine in her voice.

Blake looked past her to his brother. "What do you make of the photos? What's the point? Why deliver them now?"

Marissa wrapped thin arms around her middle. "He's been watching me for months. Some of those photos were taken in the spring."

Blake ran a comforting palm down her back.

"Can we be sure I'm the only one under surveillance?" she asked. "Is there a chance it wasn't a case of mistaken identity with the other jogger?"

The more Blake learned about Nash, the less mistakes seemed like his thing, but anything was possible. "We'll know soon."

"How?" Her voice ratcheted up, drawing the attention of several men and women in quiet discussion. "When someone else is dead?"

"No." West shook his head. "We've got no evidence to suggest he's out randomly hunting women. He's taken six in total. He's practiced. Patient and methodical. Right now, I think he's acting out on his weird cops-and-robbers fantasy with Blake."

Marissa's gaze darted up to meet Blake's.

"Nash stopped killing while I was hunting him. I lost focus on him, and he started again. I think that's why."

Marissa's heart ached. Blaming himself wasn't helping anything, but she certainly understood the inclination for self-blame. After all, she was the crowned queen of that response.

"We found the other victims," West said. "That was a huge move in the right direction, and the ME will have more details for us to go on soon." He cast a promising look at Marissa. "We're going to get Nash before he takes anyone else."

The room grunted in agreement around them.

She moved back to her place on the couch, stomach sinking further at the memory of the photos' invasive content. Marissa on a jog. Marissa at a stoplight. Buying groceries. Pumping gas. Hanging clothes on a line. She'd been so naive and vulnerable at home, rocking on the back porch while being spied on by a serial killer. Why hadn't he just taken her then? Why hadn't she sensed him there? Watching her. *Be aware. Know who's near. Look for danger.*

Her dad had spent twenty-six years drilling those lessons into her head, but she'd learned nothing.

Images of the attack screamed to mind, as bright and vivid as the moments they'd happened. He'd stalked her for months, but he'd stood out like a grizzly bear that morning. He'd dressed in the wrong clothes. Smelled like cigarettes and even spoken to her. "He made sure I saw him." Her hands grew clammy with the thought. "He could've sneaked up on me, but he made me uncomfortable on purpose." He'd wanted her to be afraid. He'd probably even counted on her not going straight to her car. If he'd followed her all those months, he had to have known she wouldn't leave the forest without a moment of reflection. She was so predictable.

Moments later, the group seemed to stand in unison and the little room bustled to life as men and women sprang toward the door with purpose.

Blake headed for her room with the little black duffel West had given him. He returned several minutes later in a T-shirt announcing Property of Cade County Sheriff's Department across the chest.

West snickered. "Looking good, Garrett."

Blake dropped his beaded chain and FBI badge over his head and screwed a black ball cap over damp, mussed hair. "No sense in aiming for sheriff, that was always in your cards."

"What I heard was that you couldn't compete."

Blake smiled at his brother with warmth and pride. The quick shower had done him well.

Marissa's earlier shower had only reminded her how sore her muscles were from yesterday's fight.

Blake braced broad hands over narrow hips and locked sharp blue eyes on her. "Ready?"

"What?" She stood, unsure why. What had she missed?

Worry etched through his brow. "I want to make another pass by Kara's place. I'd actually like to have a look inside this time. I don't suppose you or your parents have a spare key?"

"I do. At home." Her tummy bottomed out at the thought of returning to her home at night.

Blake grabbed his truck keys from the table. "We'll pick up the key on our way to Kara's. West and Cole will talk to any of her neighbors who weren't home when Cole made his rounds earlier."

"Okay." Marissa forced her body forward, collecting her phone and a light jacket from the bedroom before heading for the door.

With any luck, they'd find Kara's home just as they left it. Safe and secure. No signs of invasion. With lots of luck, they'd find Kara asleep on the couch, wiped out after a long hike and hot shower. Marissa would be content to find her at the local hospital with a twisted ankle or some other non-life- threatening injury.

Marissa strode through the hotel door with renewed hope and purpose. Maybe this was all a misunderstanding with Kara. Maybe she'd lost her phone or the battery was dead. "Here." She placed her house key in Blake's hand. "I assume you plan to go in first."

"I do." He opened his passenger door and helped her inside.

"Kara's key is on the rack in the kitchen. It's the one with the four-leaf-clover chain." She tapped the dome on his ceiling with two fingers. "Your interior light's broken."

"Disabled." He shifted into Reverse and headed away from the hotel.

"Why?"

"Stealth. Vehicles are big and loud enough without flashing a light every time I climb in or out after nightfall."

Marissa pulled her attention back to the road, unsure if the explanation was frightening or genius, and hoping there would be no need for stealth tonight.

Chapter Ten

Things were profoundly quiet outside Marissa's home. The view was exactly as she'd expected, the same one she'd enjoyed most nights for many years. An owl cocked its head at the truck as Blake eased it onto the end of her driveway. Behind the owl, soft gray clouds raced past the harvest moon, driven by the gentle breeze that worked the trees along her property line. Her fingers stretched and curled on her lap, eager to capture the shot on film, and missing her camera more than ever. A rush of fallen leaves tumbled across her lawn and adhered themselves to the narrow trunk of a baby evergreen. This night was made for bonfires and friends with spiked apple cider. Anything other than hunting a killer.

Blake shifted into Park and snuffed the headlights.

"What's wrong?" she asked. Her home was another hundred feet up the driveway, and she longed to see that it was okay. A thousand warm memories filled those walls and the acres around them. She'd give just about anything to go inside, curl beneath her grandma's quilt by the fire and pretend the last two days were nothing more than a nightmare. Sadly, her old normal was her new fantasy. Mornings of scrambling eggs in the kitchen without feeling stalked were probably gone forever, but if that was all she lost to Nash, she'd count it as a win.

His posture was rigid at her side, eyes focused and square jaw clenched.

"I thought we were in a hurry to grab the key and get to Kara's?" she asked.

He pulled his phone from the cup holder and typed something against the screen. "Your porch light is out."

"So?" She eyeballed the shadows cast from her roof over the front yard. "I haven't been home. No one was here to turn it on."

He finished prodding his phone and set the device in his cup holder. "I turned it on when we left."

Marissa pulled her attention back to Blake. "You think Nash came back here?" The photo he'd taken of her and Blake came to mind. "He was here while we were. You think he stuck around and took the bulb after we left."

"Maybe, but why?" Blake narrowed his eyes on her home. "I don't know what to expect from him anymore, which, I suppose, is exactly what he wants." He scooped her house key from the cup holder and stuffed it into the pocket of his pants.

"Are you worried?" It was hard to get a read on him when he wore that blank agent expression.

"No." He flicked his gaze to the side-view mirror outside his door. "I'm pissed."

Right. She was the worrier. He was the warrior.

The sheriff's cruiser rolled into view beside them, the headlights flashing over her home.

A great gasp tore through Marissa's chest. A figure dressed in white swung from her porch rafters. She shut her eyes shut and prayed, shamelessly, that it wasn't her sister.

BLAKE CLIMBED OUT like a ghost and shut the door behind him. He gave her a sour look and pointed through the glass. As if she needed to be warned not to follow. As if she hadn't seen enough murder victims to last her ten lifetimes.

Cole opened the cruiser's passenger door and raised a massive black flashlight at the figure. Wind whipped the thing into a near horizontal position, and Marissa let out a cry of relief. Whatever was wearing the gown wasn't human. No one weighed so little that they would float like that, not even in the force of a brewing storm.

The Garretts met in the beams of the sheriff's headlights. Together they charged toward the gown and her mysteriously darkened home. West and Blake went inside, flipping the porch light on behind them.

Cole prodded the gown as it flipped and twisted in the wind, partially filled by what now appeared to be an inflatable doll in a long blond wig.

Marissa's home illuminated room-by-room. Living room. Kitchen, bedroom, bedroom, back porch. She winced with each new light, praying that Blake was safe and Nash wasn't waiting there to surprise him.

Cole stayed in near-constant motion, patrolling the perimeter, until the others returned to view. Their silhouettes were relaxed now, knees no longer locked, shoulders slack. They'd even removed their right palms from the butts of their weapons.

Marissa strained to hear them, but they were too far away, and the winds were gaining strength, getting louder by the gust.

A tornado of emotion built in Marissa's empty stomach. If the coast was all clear, and the woman in white was only a doll, then why was she still locked in the truck? Why hadn't she been invited to join them in whatever they were discussing?"

Clouds passed over the moon, casting the men into darkness. She could see them if she squinted, but only barely. Marissa craned her neck to curse the clouds.

The loaner phone buzzed in her pocket. She freed the tiny device and checked the caller ID. Her parents' home number glowed on the screen. "Hi, Mom," she answered.

"Hi." Her mother's voice was soft. Controlled. Marissa recognized the tone immediately. She was being brave. It was the same tone she used when anyone was sick or hurt. "I'm sorry to call again. I just wanted to know you're still okay."

Marissa smiled against the receiver, hoping her effort carried though the line. "I'm good. I promise. Very safe. I'm constantly surrounded by lawmen who are all about my well-being." She forced a nervous laugh. At the moment, at least three of them were intentionally leaving her out of their conversation, but she doubted that news would make her mom feel any better. It was certainly frustrating the daylights out of Marissa. "Any word from Kara?" she asked, redirecting her thoughts. She knew the answer already, of course. If her mom had any news about Kara, she would have led with that.

"No, but I missed a call earlier. I didn't recognize the number, and there was no message. I didn't call back. Do you think I should have?"

Marissa fiddled idly with her jacket's zipper. "Probably not. If it was Kara, I think she would've left a message or kept calling until you answered." Or called Marissa. "You should tell Mr. Garrett. See what he thinks."

"Okay. I will." Her mom's voice wavered. "I made up your old room today. In case you change your mind about staying with us."

"Mom."

"I know." She sniffled. "Our old Sheriff Garrett showed up after you left. He came out of retirement for this."

"Hey," Marissa interrupted. "We're going to get through this. We'll be stronger for it."

Her mom didn't respond.

Marissa imagined her mother pressing tear-soaked tissues to her eyes and sobbing silently behind a palm. "Where's Mr. Garrett now?"

"Outside. He's been patrolling the grounds with your father ever since."

Leaving her alone. She glared at the younger

Garretts in her driveway, who were doing the same thing to her.

"I'm sorry you're alone," she told her mom. More than that, Marissa was sorry she couldn't be there to support and comfort her somehow. "I'd be with you if I could."

"I know." Her mom's careful composure was gone. "Where is your sister?" She choked the words out on a whisper. Her heartbreak split Marissa's chest in two.

"We'll find her."

Her mom's sobs flowed freely now.

Marissa would have given anything to hold her. To shoulder the burden. Her mother had lost hope, and she needed something to hold onto. "We're at my house, collecting the key to Kara's place. Blake says the house is all clear, and we're headed to Kara's next. I'm hoping she wrote her agenda on the calendar or made some other note about what she planned to do today. At least then Blake's team will know where to begin looking. I'll tell you what we find at Kara's as soon as we're finished there."

Marissa disconnected and tucked the phone back into her pocket. She'd thought yesterday was long, but today was officially worse. The hanging doll was just another attempt to scare and misdirect them, and frankly, Marissa was tired of Nash's games. It was time to get moving. Something at Kara's could be the clue they needed to bring her home.

Outside her window, growing winds bent the treetops and pushed little clouds faster through the sky.

A storm was bad news, especially if Kara was still outside somewhere. Autumn rains meant plummeting temperatures, and Kara had probably dressed in a T-shirt and pants when she left home this morning.

She reached for the door handle and froze. A shadow passed over the rearview mirror, and Marissa's senses went on high alert. She spun on her seat, twisting for a better view of the entire scene outside. She found nothing but a sheriff's cruiser and the three men still engrossed in a private meeting on her lawn. Wind whipped and pulled the fabric of their pants and jackets. The Garretts took a few lazy steps in her direction before stopping again to look back at her house.

The hairs on Marissa's neck tingled and stood at attention. A sense of urgency squeezed her heart and propelled her to act. She gripped the handle on her door and shored up her nerve, suddenly preferring to be a lot closer to the guys with guns and badges. Gooseflesh crawled up her spine as she cracked open the door and planted her feet firmly in the gravel.

The air was instantly pressed from her lungs with one powerful blow. A thick hairy arm wound over her rib cage and meaty fingers dug into the flesh of her side. A broad and calloused palm scraped against the cuts and bruises on her jaw and cheek, fingers clenching across her mouth. The stench of cigarettes overcame her.

Tears blurred her burning eyes as the unseen assailant dragged her into the shadows, her body crushed against his. Her feet twisted and flailed, unable to find purchase against her assailant's feet or shins. Her lungs burned with an increasing lack of oxygen as his palm flattened her nose and lips.

Not today, she screamed internally. *Not until I find my sister.*

Marissa's muscles tensed at the thought, and panic bled into purpose. She clutched his wrists in a powerful burst of adrenaline and bent them sharply into her abdomen and jaw until his hands shifted and his fingers loosened their grip. Marissa sucked in a fresh gulp of oxygen and screamed against his palm as he struggled to reposition his hold on her. She dug her toes into the gravel and kicked a cloud of stones at Blake's truck.

"Freeze!" Blake's strong voice bellowed through the night.

A trio of armed Garretts appeared in a flash of lightning, guns drawn. The brothers marched forward in a tight V formation. "Back away from her, Nash," Blake commanded. There was venom in his tone and vengeance in his eyes. "This is between you and me."

"And Miss Lane," Nash cooed, digging his fingers deeper into her skin.

The rebuttal from Blake's mouth was fierce and foul. He widened his stance just twenty feet away and lifted his gun higher. "You aren't getting away this time."

Marissa stopped fighting and tried to make herself smaller in case Blake planned to shoot him.

"That's a good girl," Nash whispered in her ear.

A wave of stinky breath washed over her, souring her stomach and weakening her knees. “Make him fight for you,” he said. “The agent thinks you’re his, but he can’t fight destiny forever.” He pressed his hot mouth against the tender skin along the back of her neck before curling his fingers deep into her hair and sending her headfirst into Blake’s tailgate.

The loud smack of her forehead on metal reverberated through her bones before the world went black.

Chapter Eleven

Blake's heart stopped.

Marissa's head snapped back, and her body went limp. She hit the ground in a heap.

Nash was already on the move, fleeing the scene, making his getaway.

"No!" Blake skidded in the gravel to her side. Nash could have broken her neck. She could already be gone. "Marissa!"

Footfalls pounded the earth behind him, arriving in the next heartbeat. "I've got her," Cole announced, falling onto his knees beside Blake. "Go on." His hands were already on her neck, counting her pulse.

West's silhouette raced into the woods across the street, gun drawn.

"Go," Cole insisted. "Cover West. I've got this."

Reality slapped back into focus and Blake was in motion. *Cover West.* Yeah, right. Nash was all Blake's and after what he'd done to Marissa, Blake would be damn sure he paid slowly.

He launched off the street and into the woods at a sprint, quickly catching and passing his brother.

Nash fled through the trees and underbrush ahead of them, cutting a wide path and leaving a trail impossible to miss. He was difficult to see in the darkness, dressed in black, a hoodie pulled over his head, but the sound of snapping twigs and kicked stones was a beacon guiding Blake straight to him. His ragged breathing was a bonus.

Nash was getting tired.

Blake, on the other hand, could run another half mile without slowing down, and ten miles after that before his legs grew spongy. He ran every day. Long distance. The time alone helped him think. It gave him a private place to plot Nash's demise. Now, his dreams were coming true.

Images of Marissa's bruised face challenged his concentration. The sound of her head against his tailgate. The fear in her eyes as Nash gripped her battered face in one palm and whispered into her ear. What had he said?

The overwhelming need to turn back and stand guard until the ambulance came nearly staunched his momentum. His mind and his gut were torn in two. The emotion. The confusion. These were unlike his drive to protect the public, this was like nothing he'd experienced before. It was ferocity. It was painful. And it was, he realized, a standoff between the need to stop Nash and the instinct to guard what was *his*.

For a moment, Blake had thought he'd won. He thought it was stupidity and brazen overconfidence that had brought Nash to him, but Blake was wrong.

Nash came to show Blake that he could. He could get to Marissa anywhere and beat Blake anytime.

Blake slowed his pace, and his senses sharpened. Only two sets of footfalls remained. His and West's behind him. No Nash. Based on his earlier panting, Nash must've stopped to catch his breath and hide.

Blake raised a hand to alert West, and soon his footfalls ground to a halt beside Blake. He motioned his brother to the east, then Blake turned in the opposite direction. Together, they could silently cover more ground.

The night was dark, despite the harvest moon. Gathering clouds and evergreens blocked the starry sky. Incessant winds and the rushing branch of a nearby river easily masked the huffing of Nash's breath, but he was winded, and no doubt hiding, waiting for his chance to move.

Blake wouldn't give him that chance.

A lifetime of hunting and tracking in Cade County had made Blake an apparition in the woods. Nash wouldn't touch Marissa again. Right or wrong, Blake would kill that sonofabitch the moment he had a chance.

The snapping of a nearby limb reached his ears, and Blake spun to face the sound. A shadow sprinted toward the river, and Blake pounced after it, leaping easily over fallen logs and through piles of leaves. "Freeze!" he hollered.

The panting figure continued a bumbling path toward the rushing water just beyond the cliff's edge.

Blake gained on him by the second, hope and

victory rising in his chest. Maybe he wouldn't have to kill him. Maybe he could haul Nash's sorry ass back to Marissa and let her even the score. *As soon as she wakes up*. He ground his teeth at the thought. No. This time it was Nash who would die. "Stop!" he boomed. "Or I will shoot you."

Nash skidded to a stop at the cliff's edge. There was nowhere to go but down, and if Blake remembered correctly, there was a sizeable drop on this side of the water.

Blake's eyes narrowed, moving in on Nash in small, silent strides, the way he had five years before. His trigger finger begged him to shoot and worry about the repercussions and paperwork later. Until West arrived, there were no witnesses.

Nash raised shadowy arms in surrender. "Please, don't shoot."

The plea stalled Blake's homicidal thoughts, reminding him Nash was the cold-blooded killer. Blake was the lawman. "Get on the ground. Put your hands behind your back," he barked. On his next step, Blake's boot caught on something hidden in the leaves and his heart seized. A booby-trap. The taut string pulled against his laces, and Blake launched himself away on instinct, hoping it was far enough to survive whatever came next. A ground-shaking boom blasted through the night air, rattling his teeth and jarring his bones. He crashed against the forest floor, sending shock waves of pain through his head and back. A mass of dirt and fallen limbs thundered down on him.

He wrangled his gun into position in case the attack wasn't over. The floating dust and debris complicated his newly blurred vision. The stench of tar burnt his nose.

Nash smiled. His lips moved, and he turned for the water.

Blake squeezed the trigger, getting off two shaky, half-blinded shots before the splash from Nash's plummet reached his ringing ears.

West skidded into view, giving the blast zone a wide berth. His normally tanned face was whiter than the wedding gown on Marissa's porch. "Blake!" Terror shredded his voice, raising it by octaves. "Are you hurt?" His words were garbled and hollow, but Blake raised his gun overhead and rolled back against the ground.

His brother appeared again, this time at his side peering down. "Don't move. Medics are on the way."

"Nah." He lowered his gun and reached for West's hand. "Help me up."

West hesitated before obliging his big brother. "What the hell happened?"

"The bastard set a trap. I tripped over the wire." He worked his aching joints to assess the damage. "I thought he was hiding, but he was leading me here. Now I can't decide if the strung-up doll was a setup for abducting Marissa, or if the attempted abduction was a setup to get me out here."

West dusted dirt and leaves from Blake's back and shoulders. "Did you hit him?"

"I don't know."

They inched toward the place where Nash had last stood and peered over the cliff into the dark waters below.

Sirens cried and wailed in the distance, turning Blake back in the direction he'd come. The cavalry had arrived.

"Go," West advised. "Get checked out. You're not bleeding, but that doesn't mean you aren't hurt. I've got this. My deputies are already on the way."

Blake hesitated, once again torn between his job and his heart. "There was C4 in that blast. I could smell it."

"You're lucky to be alive. Just go."

Blake swallowed painfully, and stretched his shaking limbs. "Well, watch your step."

West snorted. "I've got this. Take care of yourself and your girl."

Blake jerked into an uncomfortable jog, heart and mind racing along with his pace. It was Marissa's face he'd seen when the world blew up around him, and hers was the only one he wanted to see now. West was right. Blake couldn't be sure when it had happened or what Marissa would think of it, but the deal had been sealed in his mind. She was his girl. His to defend and protect, yes, but so much more if she'd let him.

Fierce determination powered his feet along faster. Toward the incoming sirens, the flashing lights, and Marissa. The thief who'd popped into his life, knocked him sideways and stolen his heart.

COLE'S FACE BLURRED into Marissa's view. The warmth of his body was everywhere, and the look on his face was wildly expectant.

"Ow," she groaned the first thing that came to mind. Her head and neck ached and throbbed as she struggled to recall why she was in Cole's arms instead of Blake's. And why they seemed to be sitting on the street outside her home.

He released her with one hand and raised two digits in the air like a peace sign. "How many fingers am I holding up?"

She swatted his hand away. "Why am I on your lap?" Why were they alone on the ground? Her mental wheels spun, getting nowhere.

A bright light beamed into her eyes, sending shards of pain through her skull.

She whacked blindly at the source. "What is wrong with you?"

Cole chuckled, bouncing her gently along with him. "Nothing's wrong with me. I'm trying to figure out what's wrong with you."

"What's wrong with me?" she asked.

His warm expression dimmed. "You hit your head."

"Oh." A groggy sensation crept through her bones. How had she hit her head?

"Stop fighting, and let me evaluate your injuries," Cole said, flipping the light into view again. "You could have a concussion."

She dropped her hands to her lap. "Why aren't

you a doctor?" she asked. "I remember hearing you went to medical school. What happened?"

His brows furrowed, and he averted his gaze for a long beat, as if he didn't want to answer. "That's expensive," he said finally, "and a lot more people die. I like being the hero."

She rolled her eyes and winced. "Ow."

Cole pocketed the little light. "Any nausea?"

Marissa struggled upright, easing herself away from him. "No, but my ears are ringing."

"I think that's the ambulance."

Her body tensed. The sound of metal on bone echoed through her mind. "Nash." He'd gotten to her again. She covered her mouth. There was the nausea. "Blake!" She twisted in search of him, rocking onto her knees and forcing her shaky body upright. "Holy." She pressed a hand to her head and bent forward at the waist, fighting the sickness and pain coursing through her.

"He went after Nash." Cole rose to place a steadying hand on her back.

"Where?" She lifted her face and squinted into the dark woods.

"I think you'd better sit back down."

"Where are they?" she demanded.

Cole stepped into her view. He frowned, all pretense of congeniality gone. "You were injured, and Nash ran. My brothers gave chase. You need to stay still until the ambulance gets here."

An explosion rocked the world. Marissa sucked

air and blinked through a painful bout of panic. "What was that?"

Two gunshots echoed through the night before Cole could answer.

Cole went rigid. His expression fell blank.

Marissa's stomach dropped and a whimper slipped from her lips. Tears streamed over her burning cheeks. She swallowed bile and forced five terrifying words from her mouth. "Did Nash have a gun?" She recalled his fingers mashed against her jaw. His arm around her ribs. But was he armed? Had there been a firearm under his coat? Pressed to her back?

Cole pulled her into his arms. "I don't know." The thread of worry in his voice betrayed his cool facade.

The wood line was silent, and the winds were picking up. No sounds of voices or footsteps. What was going on in there? How far had they gotten? Was Blake okay? Did he know about the cliff above the water? A knot of emotion clogged her throat and stung her eyes anew. What if she lost him? She'd only just found him.

Bright red-and-white flashes from an ambulance and several government vehicles arrived seconds later. The caravan stopped behind Blake's truck. At least two cruisers and as many black SUVs lined the space at the foot of her driveway. Multiple uniformed men and women rushed into the woods. Others paraded along the street, marking the wood line with flares and searching the ground from her driveway to the woods. Little flags were placed at boot prints in the mud. The flash of cameras and sirens mixed with a growing murmur of voices.

Cole peeled her off of him, then passed her to a man in an EMT shirt. "She has head and neck trauma. The facial abrasions are two days old. Bruising is a mix of then and now. Let's load her up. Get her out of sight while you take a look."

Marissa ran her hands over the marks on her face and neck. A flood of emotion overcame her. Fear, embarrassment, anger, humiliation. Hopefully Nash came across that cliff accidentally. "I'm not going to the hospital."

Cole snorted.

The EMT offered Marissa a concerned smile. "We don't need to go anywhere. Would you mind having a seat inside so I can make a proper evaluation?"

She eyeballed the open cargo doors. "Can we stay outside?" Her gaze ran the length of the street near the woods. "I'm fine. I don't need anything that's in there."

The man raised a stethoscope toward her in compliance, but Cole intervened.

He inched closer, nudging her toward the gaping ambulance doors. "You can barely stand up. Stop being a hero and get in so you can be checked out properly or Blake will have my ass."

She gave Cole a long appraisal. If Blake was okay, and she hoped that he was, she certainly didn't want to be another source of frustration for him. He had enough worries leading a team of federal agents and chasing a killer. "Fine, but you have to let me out as soon as you're done with your evaluation." She shuffled forward on noodle legs and struggled into the back of the ambulance. Her head swam, and she repositioned her feet for balance on the shiny metal step.

"She hasn't eaten," Cole tattled, boosting her the rest of the way inside. "The assailant threw her head-first into Blake's tailgate. She was out for about two minutes, and woke with confusion, a headache and a few moments of memory loss, but I think that's all come back to her now. She's claiming no nausea, but..." He shrugged as if he didn't believe her. "She's under severe stress. Possible post-traumatic. Her sister's missing. She's attached herself to the agent on the case, who's currently in pursuit and we just heard two gunshots."

The EMT mouthed a slow "Wow," before speaking again. "Blake's the agent?"

"Yeah."

Embarrassment rolled through her. Was that what she'd done? *Attached herself* to Blake? Was that what everyone around them saw? A victim clinging superficially to her hero? She pressed a hand to her stomach, fighting another wave of nausea. Her cheeks burned with humiliation. They'd had a near kiss at the restaurant, and the moment had meant something to her, but maybe that sort of thing was an everyday occurrence for him. She could certainly understand why if it was.

The EMT flashed another light in Marissa's eyes,

and she slapped it away. "Will everyone please stop doing that? It hurts."

He took her wrist in his fingers and checked his watch. "I'm Henry Garrett," he said. "I'm the uncle."

Marissa heaved a long breath. What was with these Garrett men? Was a hero complex in the DNA?

Cole climbed onboard and closed the doors behind him. "Uncle Henry taught me everything I needed to know about basic triage. He's the reason I pursued medical training in the army."

Henry strapped a blood pressure cuff on Marissa. "Our family requires a lot of first aid."

Marissa fixed Cole with a pleading stare. "Please find out why there were gunshots."

She fought to maintain her composure, no longer caring if everyone in Shadow Point thought she was a needy victim. All that mattered was that Blake was okay, and she needed to know that neither of those bullets had connected with him.

Cole swept his gaze to his uncle before slipping outside and shutting Marissa in.

THE AMBULANCE DOORS were shut when Blake arrived. Cole slid his phone into his pocket and lifted a palm. "I just called you."

"I didn't answer."

"I know. Why not?" He scowled.

Blake closed the distance between them in a determined stride. "Well?" he demanded, shooting a pointed look at the ambulance and fearing the worst. Why else would she be locked inside while his brother was forced out?

Cole's stance stiffened. He dropped his hand to his side. "Where's West?"

Blake reached past him for the ambulance doors. He thumped his palm against the metal. "Open up. This is Federal Agent Garrett."

Cole grabbed Blake's arm and jerked. "Where's West, Blake? Answer me." His no-nonsense tone implied there might be a fist coming if Blake didn't comply.

Blake reared to his full height and faced off with his baby brother. What the hell was wrong with him? "West's at the river. What's your problem?"

Cole stepped back, clearly relieved. "There were two gunshots and an explosion, man. What the hell do you think is my problem?"

Recognition dawned and Blake clapped a palm on his brother's shoulder. "West is fine. He's tracking Nash downstream." He dropped his hand and raised a humbled brow. "I got free of the blast, but Nash got away. Sorry man. I wasn't thinking."

Blake had been so focused on reaching Marissa that he hadn't considered what those gunshots might have sounded like to Cole. Any other day, Blake would've recognized the fear in his eyes and set the facts on the table immediately. He might've even given orders on what to do next, but at the moment all he could think about was whether or not Marissa was going to be okay.

Cole stared past Blake, confused. "You lost Nash?"

"Yeah, but I also shot him. I think. I don't know. He jumped into the river." Blake thumped the door again. "Open up."

"Jumped or fell because you shot him?" Cole asked.

The ambulance doors opened, and Blake hoisted himself inside on weakened limbs. "I don't know. Both, I hope."

"Me, too," Cole muttered, closing Blake inside.

Marissa sat on the gurney, an ice pack pressed to her head. Another drooped over her shoulder. His uncle Henry monitored an IV attached to her arm.

"You're okay?" Blake asked, falling onto the bench against the wall. His knees bumped the gurney and Marissa flinched. "Sorry."

She batted teary eyes. Her face was splotched and puffy as if she'd been crying. "What happened?"

Blake's heart broke. He abandoned the bench for a seat beside Marissa on the gurney. He pulled her to her chest and stroked her hair. "I'm so sorry I left you."

Her arms wound around his middle and his heart swelled at the touch. She buried her face against the curve of his throat and the emotions she'd so carefully hidden from him before flowed freely now. "I thought you were shot," she cried. "I thought you were blown up. Gone."

"Shh," he whispered, cradling her in his arms. "I'm okay. So is West. Verdict is still out on Nash. That was my gun you heard. The explosion was poorly rigged. I got out of the way before I was hurt." He lifted his face to search for his uncle. "How is she?"

Uncle Henry tipped his head left and right, indicating it was a draw. "It doesn't look like a concussion and the bruises will fade." He slid his gaze to a sobbing Marissa, then back to Blake with a sad smile.

Blake understood. The wounds that would take longest to heal were the ones no one could see.

"Did you get him?" Uncle Henry asked. "What did you mean the verdict is still out?"

Blake grimaced. "I tried, but he jumped into the river. West's tracking him."

Uncle Henry scooted in Blake's direction. He opened and closed his hands in the universal sign for gimmee. "Come on. Let me take your vitals and check on those cuts and burns."

Blake reluctantly stretched one arm in his uncle's direction for a pulse check and blood pressure cuff.

Someone pounded on the ambulance doors. "It's Sheriff Garrett, open up."

Blake jerked his head toward the door.

Uncle Henry waddled to the back, careful not to hit his head on the low ceiling. "All you kids with your titles. Just say, it's West. It's Blake. It's Cole. I know who you are." He pushed the doors open, and West stared inside.

"How is she?" West asked.

"She'll be okay," Uncle Henry answered. "How about the bad guy? Should I call for another bus?"

West shook his head.

"Coroner?"

"Nah. We didn't find him."

"So, I missed," Blake muttered, struggling not to upset Marissa again. Her sobs had finally fallen silent and her breathing returned to a slow and steady pace.

West raised an evidence baggie for Blake to see. There were leaves inside. "I found these on the banks near a patch of rocks and a little vomit."

Blake took the bag in one hand for closer inspection. "That's blood."

"Yep."

"I hit him."

Uncle Henry retook his seat beside the gurney and liberated a cell phone from one uniform pocket.

West cocked a hip and cast a goofy look at his uncle. "Did Blake tell you he tripped over a wire roped to some C4?"

Uncle Henry removed the blood pressure cuff and squirted something onto Blake's bloodied arm. "It's a wonder you boys haven't given your mother forty heart attacks by now. Ten for each of ya."

West rolled his eyes, then refocused on Blake. "The team's going strong. Your guys brought the lights and I've called in some of the best tracking dogs in the county. If the rain holds off, we'll have him by dawn. I'll get the leaves to the lab to confirm it's Nash's blood after the dogs get here. I'm going to stick around and direct the teams as they arrive. If you want to head back to the hotel with Marissa, we'll be okay. There's a lot of manpower in those woods chasing one injured man."

Uncle Henry shined a bright light in Blake's face.

Blake slapped it away. "Knock it off."

Marissa chuckled against his chest. Blake held her tighter, wishing he knew why she'd laughed and how to make it happen again.

"Did you check his head?" West asked. "He's talking really loudly."

Blake waved a hand over his ears. "Do not. My ears are ringing, but I can hear. My vision is fine. I'm fine. I hurt like hell, but I'll live."

Cole strode into place beside West, spotlight in hand. He tilted his head back and looked skyward. "Storm's coming. I'm heading out before it gets here. What we don't find tonight could be washed away by morning." He tipped his hat to his brothers, uncle and Marissa before jogging into the woods between flares.

Blake shifted Marissa in his arms and indicated that she should lie back on the gurney.

Shockingly, she complied.

He turned back to West. "We need to contact all the local hospitals, clinics and facilities where Nash can either get patched up or work on himself. Veterinarians and dental offices included. He's resourceful, so put the word out. It's going to be a lot harder for him to blend in while he's bleeding."

Uncle Henry wiggled his phone in the air. "I'm ahead of you, young ones."

West watched Blake. His gaze lingered on the hand, now caressing Marissa as she tried to relax.

Blake lifted his chin in response to the questions on his brother's brow.

Yes, he'd fallen hard and fast for this woman, and no, there was nothing he wouldn't do to assure Nash Barclay never got anywhere near her again.

Chapter Twelve

The walkie-talkie on West's shoulder erupted in a short blast of white noise. "Sheriff Garrett, this is dispatch," a woman's voice announced.

Marissa's eyes popped open, her body on alert. Had they found Nash floating in the river? She chastised herself for wishing that he was facedown.

West depressed the button and turned his face toward the noisy device. "Go ahead."

"I know you've got the whole team with you, sir, but there's a call about some movement outside the Lane home on Blue Grass Run. Neighbor says there's no car, but the lights are all on."

Marissa shot upright, tugging her IV and ignoring the dull thud in her head.

"Whoa." Uncle Henry shoved one hand over the tape securing her IV. "Wait a minute. Settle down."

She wiggled free of his grip. "She's talking about my sister's house. I need to go." Had enough time passed for Nash to reach Kara's place? That was nearly a mile downriver from Marissa's. She squeezed her eyes shut and tried to gauge the possibility. In a kayak, yes. On foot? Maybe, but injured? That depended on where he was shot.

She gave Uncle Henry's hand a pointed stare.

"Let the drip do its work," he insisted.

"I feel better. My head's fine. I'm not going to puke." She grabbed Blake's arm with her free hand. "Take me with you."

West left the ambulance doors open as he walked away. A moment later, the lights on his cruiser flicked on, and he maneuvered through the crush of vehicles, heading downriver toward Kara's neighborhood.

Blake looked from Marissa to his uncle.

Uncle Henry puffed his cheeks in defeat and released her hand. "She should rest. I put something mild in her IV for pain. I'd say you could leave her with me, but you've got the gun."

Blake hesitated. "I can stay. Wait for West to report back."

"No." Marissa plucked the tape from her arm and slid the needle from her vein. "I'm going. My sister could be in danger, and we already know I am. You aren't leaving me alone in this ambulance."

Uncle Henry tugged his ear. "Call me if you need me. I'm on duty all night."

BLAKE LOADED MARISSA into the cab of his truck and cursed himself for having ever left her alone there. He'd never dreamed anyone, even Nash, would try to take her with three armed lawmen a hundred feet away. Still, he'd known Nash was out there, and he'd failed to keep her safe tonight. That was all him.

She didn't speak on the drive to Kara's, and Blake's gut fisted with the fear her injuries were worse than his uncle knew. What if he'd missed something critical in his evaluation? Or maybe she was just shutting Blake out. Blaming him, with good reason, for her fear and pain. Her head lolled and rocked against the seatback as they sped down winding roads toward her sister's home. She gazed out the passenger window, effectively keeping her eyes off of his no matter how he tried to catch her attention.

He hated the silence, but couldn't bring himself to break it. Knowing now how he felt about her and what she meant to him, her quietness felt like a wall keeping him out when all he wanted was in. He shook off the selfish urge to reach for her. Marissa would talk when she was ready, but she clearly wanted space. She'd never gone so long without speaking her mind or asking a question. He gripped the wheel until his knuckles whitened, determined to keep them there. He'd give her whatever she needed, even if what she wanted was away from him.

He sped along the dark winding road as lightning splintered across the night sky, ominous and threatening. The thunder was a wild animal giving warning before each attack. Soon, fat drops of rain exploded against his windshield, winding twisty paths through his view. He hit the wipers and said a silent prayer that this was the worst of it. Too much rain would ruin the trackers' chances of finding

Nash. Even the dogs West had called in would lose the scent in a downpour.

He stole another look at Marissa, hoping she'd forgive him one day for the heartbreak he'd caused her by letting Nash live all those years ago.

A few more hills and one stop sign later, Blake pulled into Kara's driveway and parked behind West's cruiser. As promised, the porch light was on along with all the lights inside.

Marissa slid from the truck on wobbly legs. She'd been so quiet the last few moments that he thought she might've fallen asleep.

It wasn't hard to catch up with her on the path to Kara's door. "Hey, slow down." He caught her hand and pulled her back. There was no garage here, and only West's cruiser was in the driveway. Who knew what awaited them inside?

The front door swung open and another version of Marissa sprang toward them, arms open wide. The sleeves of her faded Kentucky University sweatshirt hung past her hands, and her worn-out blue jeans were torn across both knees.

Marissa shook Blake away and collided with, what could only have been, her sister hard enough to throw herself off balance.

"Whoa." He pressed a steadying palm between her shoulders.

The women rocked foot to foot as they hugged and laughed and sobbed. Wind whipped their hair and clothing. Rain pelted their cheeks.

"I'm so sorry," Kara cried. "Sheriff Garrett told

me everything you've been through and I wasn't here for you. I hate myself." She pulled back to look at Marissa's face, tears streaming from her eyes. Wild wisps of damp blond hair clung to her cheeks and forehead, the rest was swept into a messy bun and quickly falling. "Look at you." She lifted gentle fingers to Marissa's bruised face, but stopped short of touching the multitude of marks. "Oh my gosh. You didn't tell me it was this bad. What is happening?" She hugged her again and cried louder. "You said someone tried to take you. You didn't tell me he hurt you!"

Blake could see where all the emotion went in this family. Kara seemed exuberant enough for the entire town. He pressed forward, corralling them toward the steps. "Can we take this inside, please?" Nash was still out there somewhere, and if he wasn't in the process of dying, then he was hurting, pissed and looking for revenge. Kara's house wasn't far enough from where Blake had last seen him to provide any comfort. The women needed to move their reunion inside. "Let's go. Come on."

Kara pulled back again. This time to glare at Blake. "Are you the one who's supposed to be keeping her safe? The sheriff told me about what just happened. He told me you were on the way, but he didn't say she'd show up looking like this."

Blake felt the blood drain from his face. What was it with Lane women? He pushed the two in front of him toward the door. "Inside. Now."

West sat at the island of a peppy eat-in kitchen

stuffing his face with iced sugar cookies and drinking coffee. He'd hooked the heels of his boots in the rungs of a white padded bar stool and tossed his hat onto the broad laminate countertop. "So, Kara's fine," he said, munching his snack. "I got here as the coffee finished brewing." He hefted his bowl-shaped blue mug with a grin.

Marissa curled onto an overstuffed yellow couch in the adjacent sitting area and wiped her face with her palms. She pulled a furry white pillow into her arms. "Where have you been? Where's your car? Why haven't you called. Do Mom and Dad know you're okay?"

Blake stifled a smile. That was the Marissa he was used to.

Kara stretched her eyes wide. "You have no idea what I've been through today." She grabbed two hand towels from the handle of her kitchen stove and threw one to Marissa. She rubbed the other over her face and neck.

Marissa dried her face and tossed the towel aside. "I'm sure your day was awful."

"Thank you."

Blake couldn't tell if Kara's response was the result of cluelessness or sarcasm.

"I barely got out of the shower and the sheriff was at my door." She motioned to West, then poured three more mugs of coffee. "Talk about scary."

Marissa leaned forward with narrowed eyes. "He's not scary. He's here to help. Why didn't you call us back? Or return our texts? Do you know how many times we've tried to reach you? We thought you were dead." She pressed her lips tight and shot Blake a horrified expression.

Kara stepped back as if she'd been slapped. "My phone died. I told you I had to walk home. I've been gone all day. I'd already talked to both you and to Mom. You knew I was fine, and I was trying to do what you asked." She motioned to the packed bag on her kitchen counter beside a Thermos and plastic container of cookies. "I plugged my phone in the minute I walked through the front door, then I got in the shower." Kara mimed her head exploding. "I've had the worst day ever. I've only been home for like five minutes, and I've been hustling since the moment I walked in. That's *after* I was forced to abandon my car and trek like thirty miles. Now, you're here yelling because I haven't made more phone calls? The phone was dead!"

"Thirty miles? Where were you?" Marissa asked.

Kara delivered a mug of coffee each to both Blake and her sister. "Blue Ridge Byway."

Marissa gasped. "What were you doing way out there?"

"Oh, I don't know. My only sister was attacked yesterday then taken into protective custody. I was a little upset. I wanted to think, but you said it wasn't safe here, so I figured I'd better choose someplace outside of town to hike. I planned to meet you at Mom and Dad's for dinner but when I got back into town this afternoon, my gas light was on, and I had to stop to fill up." She groaned. "Of course my money was in the coozie I wrap my water bottle in, and that was nowhere to be found, so I had to go back to the park and retrace my steps until I found it. When I got back to my car the second time it wouldn't start. I had to walk all the way back to town. It was getting dark. My phone was dead. It was awful."

"You could've called from the gas station," Marissa said.

Kara shot Blake a look. "Like I didn't think of that all by myself? I did. I called Mom and she didn't answer. I couldn't remember your new federal agent cell number and your old phone isn't on."

Blake joined Marissa on the couch, prepared to stop her from saying something she might regret. He blew casual ripples over the surface of his coffee and changed the subject. "And where's your car now?"

"In the main lot at Blue Ridge Byway."

Marissa dropped her head back against the couch cushion. "What were you even doing there? I tell you I was nearly abducted by a serial killer while hiking alone, and what do you do? Get up the next day and go hiking alone!"

Kara's jaw went slack. "You said fugitive. Not serial killer, and I was trying to clear my head but you had me scared half to death, and everything was fine until I had to walk home." She made the same exasperated expression as Marissa. "Luckily, your friend's dad offered me a ride home for the last few miles."

Marissa froze, mug halfway to her mouth. "You got in a car with a stranger? Who?"

Blake fought the urge to remind Marissa that she'd done the same thing.

"I think he said you went to school with his daughter. Tammy something. He recognized me right away, thought I was you at first, actually."

Blake slid to the edge of the cushion and traded stares with West. "What'd Tammy's dad look like? What was he driving?"

"I don't know. He had a white truck. What's wrong now?" She looked to Marissa, stupefied. "I figured I was safer in a car than walking by myself straight through a town with a fugitive on the loose."

"Nash Barclay is a serial killer," Marissa growled, "and I didn't go to school with anyone named Tammy."

A powerful rumble of thunder seemed to underscore the revelation. Lightning flashed outside, illuminating the dark world for one long beat.

Blake and West were on their feet.

"How long ago did this man bring you home?" Blake asked.

Kara looked at the clock above her fireplace. "Not long. Maybe an hour? I barely had time to put cookies in the oven and jump in the shower before you guys started showing up." She rubbed her forehead and chewed her lip. "I came home. Started the coffee and cookies, packed my bag for Mom and Dad's then jumped into the shower. I planned to call you for a ride to pick up my car, and use the cookies as a bribe."

Marissa grabbed the remote and turned the television on, then flipped to the evening news. Nash's face was anchored in the corner of the frame. A line of scrolling text detailed his past kills and recent attacks, followed by a warning that he should not be approached.

Kara watched, stunned. "That's the man who drove me home."

Blake tapped the revelation into his phone, informing his team of the development as West informed his. "Nash must've dropped her off and driven the mile over to Marissa's place from here. He probably had something in mind when he removed her porch light, but we showed up and offered him something more appealing." His chosen victim seated alone in a truck.

Kara made a gurgling sound, but didn't speak. She took the remote from Marissa and pumped up the volume on her television.

West dropped his mug in the sink and stuffed his phone back into his pocket. "Cole says it's a damn torrential downpour out there, and he's calling it a night on the river search. They can't track their own paths in this." He waved a hand toward Kara's picture window. "He's heading out to meet a tow truck at Blue Ridge Byway and collect Kara's car. I'll take her to her folks' house for the night and station a deputy there to relieve Dad." He grabbed her bag off the counter and hiked it over one shoulder. "I doubt Dad will leave, but I'll try. Is this everything you need, Kara?"

She stumbled back, dragging her eyes from a

news clip time line of Nash's kills. She turned for her kitchen on shaky legs. "Let me grab the cookies."

Marissa heaved herself off the couch and met her sister at the island. "I'm sorry." She wrapped Kara in her arms and hooked her chin on her shoulder. "So. So. Sorry. And so glad you're okay. I should have led with that. I took this all out on you, and I was wrong. You couldn't have known." She hugged her sister tight.

Kara shook visibly in Marissa's embrace.

Blake ground his teeth and headed back outside to patrol the perimeter while the women said good-bye. If Nash was brave enough to have followed them here, it would be the last place he ever visited.

Chapter Thirteen

Marissa adjusted the vents in Blake's dash to dry her rain-soaked hair. Her heart was lighter, knowing Kara was safe, but having her back meant having her to lose, and she suspected that fear would never truly leave.

Rain pelted the windshield as they followed West's cruiser toward the stop sign at the end of the street. West turned right, taking Kara to their parents' home for safekeeping, and Blake idled his truck.

He glanced at Marissa before pressing the left turn signal. "She's going to be okay."

"How do you know?" Marissa watched as the cruiser's taillights faded into the night. The fear of never seeing Kara again knotted in her muscles. "How can you be sure Nash won't show up at my parents' house and hurt them?"

Blake made the turn, pointing them soundly away from Kara. "For one thing, I know he's hurt. For another, we both know he likes to abduct and overpower women when they're alone. Kara's not going to be alone again until he's caught. She has no reason to sneak away in a storm, and she'll be safe inside. He's not a home invader, and if he gets the notion to try, he'll find three armed men inside."

Marissa appreciated the logical explanation and the way Blake always took the time to fill her in instead of blowing off her concerns. He trusted her to handle the truth. As he should.

Wind whipped the trees along the road's edge, bending boughs fifty feet high. The storm had been in full force when they'd left Kara's house. Even the short run down her drive had been enough to soak them. Now, not only was she freezing, she was worried. The search for Nash had been called off due to weather.

She twisted a loose thread from her jacket cuff around her trembling fingers. There were too many questions and her eyelids were growing heavier by the second. Her adrenaline was long gone, and whatever was in her IV was starting to wear off.

"Hey." Blake stole a long look in her direction. "Why'd you quit fighting back there?"

"When?"

"Nash had you, and you were making headway toward freedom, but when we got to you, you froze. Was it the guns? None of us would have taken a shot with you there like that. Your safety is always number one."

She rolled her eyes in the dark cab. "I wanted you to shoot him. I was trying not to get in the way."

The truck slowed for several seconds before powering onward at the posted speed limit. Whatever Blake thought about her reasoning, he didn't say.

She forced her tired eyes open, and ran mentally through a growing list of concerns. Where was Nash now? How injured was he? Would he survive? Would he come for her again? For her sister? Someone else? Images of the women pulled from the lake came flashing back to mind, curling her fingers and knotting her empty stomach. He had to be stopped, but how? What could she do? Nothing. Nash proved that time and again. She was helpless, and he could reach her anywhere, even in her driveway with three armed men standing on her lawn.

Blake pulled into the parking space outside their hotel room and turned off the lights. How had they gotten there so fast? An agent exited the door to their room, just like before. This time, the man in the suit headed for Blake with a large umbrella overhead.

Marissa waited, too exhausted to get out, wishing she could just sleep where she was.

Blake took the umbrella and sent the agent away. He arrived at Marissa's door a moment later and reached for her hand.

"You know we're both already soaked, right?" She smiled and planted her hand in his.

He pulled her against him under the large black dome and shut the door behind them.

She shook her head, pushing away the bizarre fantasy that the small gesture meant something more than good manners. Cole's words to his uncle blared in her memory like a humiliating foghorn.

She'd attached herself to him. The connection she imagined wasn't real.

Marissa headed for the bathroom once they were safely inside. She pulled a dry towel off the rack and pressed it against the length of her hair, then patted her face.

Blake leaned against the doorjamb between her room and the sitting area, watching her through the open bathroom door.

She rubbed the towel against the gooseflesh rising on her arms. "I'll only be a minute."

"Take your time."

She closed the door and hurried through the process of washing Nash's touch from her skin. It was pointless work. Each time the washcloth passed over a part of her that had touched him, her stomach knotted, and the sound of his voice burned in her ear. His breath was on her cheek. The scent of cigarettes seemed to float on the steam around her.

A bone-jarring sob broke from her, and she turned the shower off with a snap. She dried and redressed quickly, barely removing the water from her hair and skin. She wrapped half-dry hair into a messy bun and let her clothing stick to still-damp skin. She just needed to see Blake was there, and she wasn't alone.

She reopened the door to find Blake in the same location, poised between rooms. His gaze kept a steady circuit from the front door to the bedroom and back.

"You're up," she said, tossing her duffel and wet things into the closet.

He tapped his phone screen, then gave her one stiff nod.

He disappeared into the bathroom, and Marissa exhaled long and slow. She hadn't been alone since her morning jog at the national park, but the suite felt safer somehow than the small bathroom had. She was less vulnerable. There was room to run. Lamps to throw. She circled the rooms checking the window and door locks. All secure. As she expected. Two agents stood outside the front window with giant umbrellas. "Well, that explains his last-minute text," she muttered, simultaneously thankful and concerned by the added protection.

Steam puffed beneath the bathroom door and scents of Blake's shampoo filtered into her troubled mind. She turned for the front room in search of the minifridge and a cold bottle of water. Anything to help clear her thoughts.

She climbed onto the small sofa with her drink and folded her legs beneath her. She dialed her mother's number and waited impatiently for an answer.

"Hello? Marissa?"

"Hey." She swiped a renegade tear from her cheek. "Did Kara get there okay?"

"Yes."

The joy and relief in her voice raised a smile on Marissa's lips. "Good." She nodded against the receiver. "And there's a deputy there now? Someone should be staying with you tonight."

"That's right." Her mother sniffled. "We have a

full house. Mr. Garrett is staying and so is his youngest son and another deputy."

"Cole's staying?" Marissa asked.

"Mm-hmm." The background voices grew louder. "The sheriff dropped her off and waited for the deputies to arrive, then he had to go. I'm serving coffee now. I wish you were here."

"Me, too," Marissa admitted. It would be great to crawl into her childhood bed and sleep soundly knowing her parents were right down the hall, and that they were all the protection she needed. Maybe she could do that again one day, but this wasn't the night. Tonight, the whole family needed a team of guardians because one psychopath liked killing people who looked like the Lane women.

"Are you okay? Is there anything I can do?"

Marissa scanned the impersonal room before her, full of files, frequented by strangers and void of any personal touch. "No. I'm fine. I was just checking on you and Kara. I'm going to get some sleep."

Her mother sighed. "The last two days have been horrific for me. I can't imagine what they've been for you."

"I'm fine."

"You always are." Her voice was soft like a hug. "Tomorrow will be a better day. You and your sister are safe now, and that's all that matters. The whole sheriff's department can move into the guest room permanently for all I care, so long as I know my girls are okay."

The bathroom door opened, and Blake emerged in

a black t-shirt and jogging pants. His hair was damp, and his skin red from the hot shower.

Marissa gripped the phone a little tighter. "Tell Dad and Kara I love them. I'll talk to you in the morning."

"You'd better. I love you, sweetie."

"I love you too." Marissa disconnected and set the phone aside, letting her mother's comforting words warm her bones.

Blake pulled an extra blanket from the closet and carried it to the couch. "May I?"

"Sure."

He fanned the blanket over her legs and took a seat beside her. "Checking in on your family?"

"Yeah. They're fine. Your dad, Cole and another deputy are all staying there tonight."

"Good. I don't think they need the coverage, but their presence should help your family sleep. They've all had a bad day." He bent to retrieve a fat stack of files, then balanced them on his lap.

Apparently, he had more work to do.

Marissa pulled the blanket up to her chin. "Why'd Nash drive Kara home tonight? Why didn't he take her or hurt her while he had the chance?"

Blake turned his heavily burdened gaze on her. "Nash doesn't want her. This isn't random for him. He's specific. Focused. Exact. He wanted to send us a message. He wants us to know he's done his research. He's watched you. He knows what's important to you, and he wants you to know he's in control. He may have even let you get away from him at the national park because that was the surest way to get me involved."

Marissa's jaw dropped. "You think he let me go?" She pressed her fingers to the pulse suddenly beating in her temple. "I fought like hell to get away from him."

Blake lifted a palm slightly off the folder. "It's just a theory."

She frowned. The storm rumbled outside the window, rattling the glass and whistling around the door. Sheets of rain streaked over the large pane of glass beside her as if they were slowly being submerged. "Anything else you want to share?"

Blake eased the top folder in her direction and flipped the cover open. "Yes."

HE SLID THE open folder onto her lap and watched as she began to read.

Time moved more slowly as she pored over the pages, catching his eye from time to time when the messy scrawl on sticky notes became too much to decipher. She tapped her finger to the letters *BF* scribbled in a margin note.

Blake cleared his throat and began to explain the context. "It was to remind me to find his birth father." Nashville Levi Barclay was the child of a single, teenage mother. No father was named on his birth certificate. "I've always wondered about his true paternity. One-night stand? Rape? Incest?"

Marissa's mouth turned down on both sides. "Do you really think it could be one of the latter?"

"I never found out. I know he was raised in poverty by his grandparents who weren't real thrilled by the burden. I had the significant displeasure of meeting with them after he got away from me the first time. They described him as an ungrateful child, and they believed in corporal punishment. His mother was absent. I got a good idea of why while I was there."

Marissa leaned back against the couch cushions. "His life sounds terrible. No child should grow up feeling unloved or unwanted."

Blake twisted to face her. He'd decided in the shower that he'd tell her as much as he could. She deserved to know what he knew. "Nash had a relatively productive life for a while. He finished high school. Got a job and met a girl. They were engaged to be married, but she died of a drug overdose before the wedding. She left a vague suicide note. That was six years ago, and what I see as his breaking point."

She stared at the pages. "He was going to have a family. He had someone who wanted him, but not enough to keep living."

"I'd thought that Nash's first victim went missing a year after his fiancée's death." Blake stopped to rub the back of his neck and groan. "That's another thing I was wrong about. One of the bodies from the lake was a year older than that."

Marissa looked ill. "So, he'd actually started killing right away," she whispered.

"Maybe. I'll know more when I get the medical examiner's official report." Until then, everything he thought about what Nash had done to the victims was pure speculation, including the events on the day he killed them. Blake dropped his hands onto his lap and rubbed his palms together. "I think he attacked you and killed that jogger because I stopped trying to find him." Sickness coiled in his gut. He glanced at Marissa, wary of what he'd see in her expression. "I'd put his case aside and resolved to make myself useful on active criminal cases. Then, this happened. I don't think the timing is a coincidence."

Marissa raised an eyebrow. "You think he somehow knew you'd stopped looking for him?"

Blake watched her carefully as he answered. "I think so. Yes."

Someone knocked at the door. "Room service," a familiar voice called.

Blake hoisted himself upright and went to check the peephole. "While you were in the shower, I put in a request for some food." An agent with a bag of takeout and a giant umbrella stood at attention in the rain.

Blake thanked his teammate and accepted the meal before engaging the door chain and dead bolt once more.

Marissa pushed the files onto Blake's empty seat and rubbed her eyes.

"Any more questions?" he asked.

"Why do you do this?"

Blake set the bag on the couch and dropped the stack of files onto the floor. "I thought there should be food here if you got hungry. We know Kara's safe, so now maybe you can eat."

Marissa pulled the bag onto her lap and extracted a salad and cup of dressing. "I meant, isn't it hard to always be on the prowl for a monster? The people you go after are the worst of humanity, and I never gave them a second thought until yesterday. Not you, though. You chose this as your life." She popped the lid on her container, looking baffled. "You all do."

Blake moved the bag to the floor. He'd heard this before. "By all, I assume you mean my brothers and I."

"Well, yeah, and your dad. You've all chosen careers like this. Isn't it lonely and exhausting?"

"Tell me how you really feel," he joked. "Please don't hold back."

Marissa smiled. "I'm just trying to understand."

"Some families sing or sail or own horses. Garretts protect and serve."

"And you all enjoy it?"

Blake took his time answering. Marissa wanted to know him, and he didn't want to mess it up. "I think so. I do. I grew up in awe of my dad and uncles. They're all patriots and veterans, and I wanted to honor that by emulating it. So, I followed their paths to the military after high school graduation. All my brothers did, too."

"I think that's beautiful," she said. "Did you learn a lot in the service that helps you today?"

"I learned the importance of self-discipline, and I got a look at how bad life can be for some folks. Before that, I'd assumed my life in Shadow Point was the basic, standard issue stuff. I'd had no idea how great I had it here. I came home with a phenomenal appreciation for the freedom and profound safety in a rural American town. I knew I wanted to be a federal agent. I wanted to make more towns as secure as ours." He barked a humorless laugh. A lot of good he'd done.

Marissa worked through her salad, bite by greedy bite. "You wanted to make a difference," she said, pointing her fork in his direction.

He gripped the arm of the couch and tried to look less horrified at the amount of personal information he was unloading. "I know I'm not going to change the world. I don't have the tools or capacity to cure cancer or end wars, but I can do my part to protect the lives of my cases."

Marissa shifted her attention from her dinner to Blake's eyes. "I think what you're doing is noble. Most people wouldn't risk their lives to improve the lives of others."

He shifted in his seat, focusing wholly on Marissa. "I won't let him touch you again."

She pushed a hunk of lettuce with the plastic tines of her fork. "This isn't your fault. No matter how it feels to you."

Blake turned his face away. That was the kind of line he was supposed to give struggling victims and not the other way around. "Right."

"Do you ever miss normal?" she asked. "Ever

wish you had a safe job counting beans or raising chickens or something?"

"I hate chickens."

She laughed. "No. Why?"

"Chickens are mean."

"Chickens are adorable." Marissa took another bite and chewed slowly. "Why do you think none of your brothers have ever married? Seems like having a family would be great for people like you." The color in her cheeks deepened. "You'd have people to care for twenty-four seven. Not cases or strangers, but *your* people."

She made it sound so simple. Blake teetered over the right way to answer a complicated question. "I shouldn't speak for my brothers, but I think we'd all like to have a family one day. Lord knows our mom would love to have some women around. She wanted one girl and got four boys."

Marissa set her fork aside and rested her hands in her lap, looking profoundly uncomfortable. "You all want families, but none of you date." Her eyebrows knitted together.

Blake had fielded these types of questions all his life, and they never got easier. The assumptions people made always seemed to reflect poorly on him or his character, and a few years back he stopped trying to explain himself, and started throwing snide responses to keep people from pushing. The remarks had gotten a lot of lip service and their impact had stained his brothers, too.

He worked his jaw. He wanted Marissa to understand him, even if she didn't like what she heard. "I've never been married because women don't respond well to being left alone for indefinite, sometimes frequent, periods of time where I care for other women." He motioned around them. "Alone in hotel rooms."

Her eyes widened. "I can't imagine being with someone I didn't trust completely, but even then, trusting strangers with the most important person in your life is a whole other problem. That must be hard." She wrinkled her nose in distaste. "You've been more than a comfort to me. Are you always this involved with the victims?"

Did he always hold their hands and embrace them as often as possible? Was that what she thought? He struggled to hold back a deeply frustrated groan. "No."

He rubbed his hands against his thighs. Discussing all the times he'd been dumped for choosing work over a personal life wasn't exactly easy, and the look on her face made it infinitely harder. "The women in my past have also taken issue with the number of secrets I have to keep and the injuries I regularly acquire. When I'm really unlucky, the secrets and injuries come in an inconvenient two-for-one package." He lifted cautious eyes to hers, and wondered again if Marissa was the kind of woman who could withstand life with a lawman. "I'm single because I stopped dating the minute I realized none of it would ever lead anywhere as long as I am who I am, and I like who I am."

Marissa's wide eyes grew inexplicably sad. "I like who you are, too." She set her half-eaten salad on the floor and tipped over, leaning her head against Blake's shoulder. She slid her arm under his and bent it to lock them together. "I think you're a brave and selfless man who risks his life to save others, and that's pretty amazing. I'm..." A long yawn interrupted her words. "I'm glad you're the one here with me tonight."

Blake's heart expanded until he thought it'd break his ribs. He wiggled free from Marissa's grip and wrapped his arm around her back, pulling her closer and repositioning her head on his chest where she'd be more comfortable. He twined the fingers of his free hand with hers and gently kissed the top of her head.

Maybe he was asking for heartbreak by hoping there could be a future with this woman, but damn it, a prize like that was worth the risk.

Chapter Fourteen

Marissa woke to the din of buzzing voices and scents of hot coffee, scrambled eggs and sausage. Someone had left a glass of orange juice on her nightstand beside a plate with an apple and enormous cinnamon muffin. Her tummy groaned at the sight of everything. She swung her feet over the bed's edge and arched her back in a gentle stretch.

This was the time of day when her limbs longed to run. She worked her neck carefully side to side, assessing the damage and lingering ache in her head after being knocked out by Nash. She winced as her muscles locked down in defense against the movement. Too far. Too soon. Maybe after she found out what all the commotion was about, she could locate an ice pack and some painkillers.

She gulped the juice and bit into the muffin before sliding bare feet onto the floor. An angel had also left a bottle of aspirin. She took a pair of those, too.

Beyond her bedroom, the sitting area buzzed with chatter. She padded closer and peered through the opening where Blake had left the door ajar. Two agents and a deputy took phone calls around the small table. Blake's palms were braced on either side of a topographical map. He was dressed in cargo pants, boots and a fitted long-sleeved black compression shirt. His badge swung over the image, as if it too was attempting to locate something.

Or someone.

"You found him," she said breathlessly.

Blake's head jerked up, and his gaze fell immediately upon her. He cut the distance between them with a look of excitement and purpose in his eyes. "Good morning," he said softly.

Her toes curled into the carpet. "Hi."

"How'd you sleep?"

"Okay, considering. Thank you for putting me in bed. I barely remember getting there." She'd fallen asleep on the couch with his strong arms around her and her head on his chest for a pillow. She hugged her middle, embarrassed by the happiness that memory brought her.

"I wouldn't have moved you, but your neck..." He trailed off. Blake moved slightly to one side, blocking her view of the sitting room, successfully erasing everything except Blake and his intoxicating energy. "How are you feeling this morning?"

She forced a tight smile. "I'm fine. My neck's a little stiff. Thank you for the breakfast and aspirin."

His lips curved into a prideful smile.

"I mostly feel lucky. I've had a lot of prayers answered these last two days."

"You're about to get one more."

"Why? What's going on?" She glanced past Blake toward the map and men in the next room. Something big must have brought them there and gotten Blake so wound up.

"Dispatch got a viable tip on Nash at dawn. Someone saw a man fitting his description at the national park. He said the man appeared sick or hurt." His eyes lit with the final report.

"You think it's really him?"

"West is there now. Park rangers checked it out first and found a pretty heavy blood trail on the forest side of the lake."

Marissa pondered the reasons Nash would return to the lake, but only found one. "He's dying. I bet he wanted to be with the women again." But they were gone now, no longer his sick trophies in an underwater tomb. Now, they would be laid to rest properly, given the peace and respect they deserved. "Would he drown himself to be with the women?" Wouldn't he know they were already gone?

Blake rubbed his palms against her arms, then curled long fingers around her biceps. Excitement pulsated off him. "I don't know, but I told West I'd meet him. I'm leaving a deputy with you. He'll be outside, so you can take your time having breakfast and getting ready to go home." He smiled at her. "I've been waiting a long time for this."

Marissa rocked onto her toes and wrapped her arms around his neck. She'd miss Blake terribly when he returned home to Louisville, but capturing Nash was all that really mattered now.

"Moving out," a man barked from the sitting room, and the area burst into a flurry of activity. Papers rustled and chairs bumped against the floor.

Marissa turned her mouth to Blake's ear. "Go get him," she whispered.

The front door opened and closed with a thud. "Let's go, Garrett," the same deep voice from her sitting room, now bellowed outside.

Marissa rested her palms against his chest. "This is it, Agent. Your time to shine."

Blake was motionless. His grip on her tightened, and the look in his eyes nearly stole the breath from her body.

"Kiss for luck?" he asked. His gaze moved hotly from her eyes to her lips.

"Yes," she breathed.

He raised his warm hands to cradle the back of her head, and he lowered his lips over hers. "Yeah?" he whispered against her mouth.

"Yeah." The heat from his touch moved through her bones, electrifying her skin and pooling in her core. She curled her fingers into the fabric of his shirt and melded herself to him in confirmation. Blake deepened the kiss with a rumbling exhale, engulfing her in his strength and making delicious promises that he couldn't stay long enough to keep. She reveled in the taste and feel of him, trailing her hands over his shoulders and winding her fingers into his hair.

Blake ended the kiss far too soon, leaving her weak-kneed and woozy. A haze of desire lingered in his eyes. "We should probably talk about that when I get back."

She brushed careful fingertips over still tingling lips. "Then, hurry."

A broad smile spread over Blake's handsome face. "Yes, ma'am." He grabbed his black jacket, then Marissa once more. "I'm finally going to put this devil in handcuffs." He kissed her nose and forehead. "Don't go anywhere."

In the next moment, he was gone. Marissa watched as he strode through the door and joined a caravan of waiting cruisers and black government vehicles in the parking lot.

As promised, one deputy remained outside her door.

Marissa collapsed on the bed, reliving the perfect moment. Her heart had pounded so hard, she was sure Blake could feel it in his own chest. She'd waited all her life to be kissed like that. It wasn't awkward, or polite and uncertain. It was passionate and comfortable and confident. Blake had kissed her with ease and familiarity, as if they'd kissed a hundred times before. As if he already knew what she wanted and how to give her exactly that.

She closed her eyes to savor the precious thought, but slowly, reality set in, raising her eyelids and putting her back on her feet. Nervous energy filled her mind with every form of worst-case scenario. She checked her phone for missed texts, then sent a few to her mom and sister letting them know that all was well. Nash was in the cross hairs, and she'd tell them more as soon as she knew something.

Both women responded within seconds, sending return texts of love and gratitude, complete with heart emoticons. Kara was clearly rubbing off on their mother.

With nothing to do but wait, Marissa finished her breakfast and helped herself to two cups of black coffee, then cleaned up. The clock seemed to stand still as she made the bed and returned the spare blanket from the couch to the closet. How long did it take to track a dying man through the forest in broad daylight? Blake and the team had been gone more than an hour already.

An ominous feeling crept over her, and she peeked between the curtains to be sure her detail was still standing guard.

She was overthinking. Worrying. Confusing the awful things that she'd experienced over the past few days with what was happening now.

She carried her loaner phone into the bathroom and climbed into a raging hot shower hoping Blake would call before she finished getting ready. The pulsing water and thick steam slowly unknotted tension in her neck and shoulders, but the temporary escape from her thoughts didn't last.

She dug through her bag of hodgepodge clothing, smashed together and wrinkled beyond recognition. The day she'd hastily gathered those things seemed like something she'd seen in a movie rather than a moment she'd been part of. Of course, Blake had been right to insist she go into his protective custody. Nash had been watching her even then. Standing right outside her window, taking photos and stalking silently from the tree line.

She swept a dose of mascara over her eyelashes and dotted gloss on her lips. Blake and West knew what they were doing, and so did their teams. They would get Nash, and the worst part about today would be saying goodbye to Blake when the case was closed.

Marissa wandered to the couch and checked on the deputy again before turning on the television. Maybe the local newscasters had information that she didn't. Any form of update would go miles toward settling her worried heart.

A commercial for a local burger joint was cut short by the Breaking News logo. Marissa pulled her feet onto the couch and crossed her fingers for good news. Maybe even an image of Blake and West hauling their bleeding nemesis from the forest.

Instead, fire trucks filled the screen and the news anchor bobbed into view outside an inferno. "I'm here at the Winchester Farm where a propane tank explosion has rocked several acres and a number of nearby homes. The tank exploded suddenly while the family worked in a neighboring field. First responders can be seen administering triage, but there's no official word on the number of injured or severity of their burns. The Winchesters' youngest child, Emma Grace, has gone missing in the chaos and local deputies are searching the area on foot for signs of the missing toddler."

The camera panned from the reporter's face to the mess behind her.

"Hey!" Marissa scolded the screen. She squinted at the line of deputies moving slowly through the tall grass field. Those guys were supposed to be at the national forest helping Blake. The idea that this timing was too poor to have not been choreographed niggled in her mind.

She swiped her phone off the couch, and dialed Kara. "Tell me you're okay," she demanded at the sound of her sister's voice.

"Mom's making me crazy," Kara scoffed. "I just showed her my driver's license to confirm my age is not ten."

Marissa turned on her knees for another look at the deputy outside. "Are you watching the news?"

"It's all we watch here."

Marissa's knee bobbed and her intuition spiked. "Do you think there's any way the fire could be related to Nash?"

"Which one? The Winchesters' or the Caswells'?"

"What?" Marissa scooted to the edge of her seat and increased the television volume. "What happened to the Caswells?"

"Barn fire."

Sure enough, the scrolling feed along the bottom of Marissa's screen covered a barn fire a mile or two from the propane explosion. If they were Nash's doing, at least the national forest and both fires were across town from the hotel where she was hiding. Blake and West were still close enough to get him.

"So, they just left," Kara finished.

Marissa had missed the rest. "What? Who left?"

"Weren't you listening? I said the Garretts left. The dad and the deputy. The Caswells are good friends of theirs and the wife was hurt. Then, the deputy who stayed behind left ten minutes later to go help look for the Winchesters' toddler."

Marissa's stomach knotted. There was no way this was a coincidence, not when Blake had just taken a team into the national park. "I wish they hadn't left you alone." She couldn't bring herself to be angry with the men who'd left her parents' house. What else could they do when lives were in immediate danger? They had to go.

"Maybe you should come here," Kara said. "Ask your detail to bring you over before he gets called away, too."

Marissa nodded. She should talk to the deputy. Make sure he would take her somewhere else if he was needed at the scene of another crime or tragedy. At the very least, he could check in with Blake and West about what to do. She certainly didn't want someone else to be denied the help they needed because she was monopolizing a deputy.

She hoisted herself upright and stuffed her feet into sneakers, then tossed a jacket over the crook of one arm. "Let me see what he says, and I'll call you back."

"You'd better," Kara said. "I love you."

"Love you." Marissa disconnected and steadied her nerves. If Nash had drawn all the lawmen away so he could come for her, would this deputy be able to handle him on his own? Nash had escaped Blake twice. He was smart enough to have possibly created this elaborate web of confusion for authorities. She peeked at the deputy once more. Maybe it would help if the deputy came inside instead of standing guard at the door like a neon sign announcing her whereabouts.

A worrisome chill filtered through her thoughts once more. Had Nash already come for Blake? Had he lured him into the forest to kill him?

Slowly, her world began to tilt and spin. Nash could be anywhere. He could be out there, hurting the people she loved, and there was nothing she could do about it. Except, come inside and barricade the door. There was still strength in numbers.

She unlocked the dead bolt and turned the knob.

The door snapped against her chest, knocking her into the wall and onto the floor.

Nash marched over the threshold with a sick, smug-looking smile. "Hello, lovely."

Chapter Fifteen

Blake stepped carefully through the fallen leaves of the national park, determined not to lose Nash's trail or destroy evidence with haste. He and West had parted ways with their teams, fanning out to cover more territory when the blood had seemed to disappear completely. Blake's agents had entered the forest two miles away, where the river behind Marissa's house met the national park. If the intel was good, covering the area in every direction was certain to result in Nash's capture.

Maybe Nash had stopped to suture himself when he'd gotten deep enough into the trees. Maybe the injury wasn't as bad as Blake had hoped, and the bleeding had simply stopped with enough continued pressure. Whatever had happened, Blake hadn't seen a drop of blood in twenty minutes despite his sweeping arch path and trained eye.

He'd moved on to looking for evidence another human had recently been this way. Footprints. Broken limbs. Dropped items. Thread caught in the brush. Following Nash through the woods to the river had made one thing abundantly clear. Nash was not a woodsman.

Blake stopped to zip his coat higher and unwrap a stick of chewing gum. The temperature was dropping, and he needed to think. "Where are you?" he whispered.

A cluster of mismatched branches caught his eye. He squinted through the hazy mist of cold autumn rain. Even in the densest part of the forest, the configuration wouldn't occur naturally. The leaves were from different trees.

Hope rose in Blake's chest, and he scanned the area for West or a deputy, but found neither. He drew his gun and crept toward what appeared to be a hunting blind or makeshift shelter. Hunting was prohibited in the national park, so Blake's money was on the latter, likely crafted by a shifty fugitive whose face had been plastered over the local news.

"Nash Barclay," Blake announced, throwing his voice so that West and his deputies were certain to hear. He secured himself behind the width of an ancient oak, and positioned his weapon against the rough bark, lining up the best shot. "Show yourself."

Crunching leaves and heavy footfalls sounded in the distance.

Blake shored his aim and tried once more to coax the killer out. "This is Federal Agent Blake Garrett. You are under arrest. Come out with your hands where I can see them, then get down on the ground so I'm not tempted to shoot you again."

West appeared several moments later, gun drawn

and moving stealthily toward the flimsy structure. A sharp whistle cut through the biting autumn air. West waved a hand overhead. "Empty." West kicked a line of evergreen branches loose, revealing the structure's interior.

Blake moved to his side, disgusted at another miss on the monster. He toed through the mess, previously hidden by the branches. A medical kit and food rations were visible among a pile of ratty blankets and gallon jugs of water.

"Back here," West called from outside the shanty.

Blake stepped over the items, certain to be covered in Nash's fingerprints and DNA.

A fallen deer lay behind the structure, gutted and carefully covered in leaves.

Gutted. Blake turned in a circle, debating whether or not to scream until the mountains fell or just lose his mind silently. "This is the trail of blood we've been following? A deer?" He cursed silently as the steady trickle of occasional raindrops grew into the steady patter of a budding shower.

West didn't bother answering the obvious. Instead, he moved in for a closer look at Nash's possessions, including a pile of papers under a blanket with foodstuffs. "We've got more photos of Marissa and Kara in here." He swore under his breath. "Newspaper clippings about the missing jogger he killed."

Blake fought to stay focused. They needed a new plan. Nash had led them to his little hideout? Why would a fugitive do that? He cast his gaze through the forest around them. None of his team or the other deputies had arrived yet. Were they all too far away to hear his voice like West had, or were they all in trouble? "Where is everyone?"

West cocked a hip and rubbed his forehead. "I had to send my guys to the Caswells'. Dispatch called in a barn fire. Mrs. Caswell's hurt. The barn's a loss. The fire's giving Shadow Point FD a mess of trouble."

"Caswells?" Blake repeated. "Mom and Dad will want to check on them."

West grimaced. "They do. Dad already sent the text. He and Cole headed that way about thirty minutes ago. Mom's meeting them there."

Blake stiffened. "Who's with the Lanes?"

"No one for now. My other man had to help at the Winchesters'. Their propane tank exploded, and their little girl's missing. I had to send everyone there who wasn't at the Caswells."

Blake turned on his heels and began the long run back to his truck. "Nash set those fires."

West fell into step beside him.

Blake called his team. "Get back to the hotel," he instructed. "This was a ploy to get us away from Marissa. What's your position?"

He hung up and dialed the deputy stationed outside her hotel room door. "No answer," he growled. "My men were halfway here, and now they're backtracking to their vehicles before they can get en route to the hotel. Your damn deputy isn't answering."

"We don't know this was Nash," West called.

Blake slowed to glare at his brother. "How long have you been the sheriff?"

"Four years."

"And when was the last time every one of your men were called out at once?"

West ran faster. "Never."

Blake's truck sprayed gravel through the parking lot before West reached his cruiser. He redialed Marissa's loaner phone a half dozen times. "Damn it!" He smacked the wheel. "Call Marissa."

Again, the call went to voice mail.

He crushed the gas pedal underfoot and gripped the steering wheel until his fingers ached from the effort. His heart banged and flopped as wildly as his windshield wipers cutting through frigid rain.

Ten long minutes later, Blake arrived at the hotel, having broken every traffic law for the past seven miles. He rocked the truck to a stop outside the open hotel room door and jumped from the cab.

The deputy was down. Blake stayed low as he hustled to the fallen man's side and pressed two fingertips against the cold skin of his throat in search of a pulse. A rush of relief coursed through him at the feel of a steady beat beneath his fingertips. The deputy would live, but the group was in trouble. His walkie-talkie was missing, and Blake didn't have to guess where it had gone.

Blake stretched onto his feet and braced his back against the wall outside the partly open hotel room door, then kicked it wide. "FBI!"

He stormed the rooms, clearing them one by one. The place was empty but tossed. Someone had thrown all the lamps and broken one. Marissa hadn't left the room without a fight. Blake could only hope she wasn't out cold now, like the deputy.

Blake called the paramedics, then began a more calculated search of the room. "Where did you take her, Nash?" he whispered.

Her jacket and purse lay on the carpet near the door as if she'd planned to go somewhere. He said a silent prayer that she'd made it out on her own, that maybe she'd taken Nash down with the busted lamp and left him to lick his wounds like she had in the forest.

He dialed her phone again, a bubble of hope rising in his chest. They could trace her phone. Even if she wasn't answering, they could find her as long as the phone stayed on.

A phone rang several feet away. He kicked Marissa's jacket aside and watched the abandoned device pulse and vibrate on the floor, extinguishing the last of his hope.

The deputy moaned, drawing Blake's attention. He dialed West on his way back outside. "Your man's down, but alive. Looks like head trauma. Nash took his walkie-talkie. He'll be listening. Paramedics are on the way for this one."

"Marissa?" West asked, the engine of his cruiser growling in the background.

Blake swallowed a brick of emotion and rubbed

the deep ache in his chest. “Gone.” Of all the things he wanted to say, that seemed all that mattered. He rolled his eyes skyward, searching a soaring sea of evergreens. *Where are you, Marissa?*

A shrill and distant sound echoed through the trees. Blake’s muscles tensed. He turned his head in search of the scream as it came again, louder this time. He moved into the lot and craned his neck for a better look at the towering mountains behind the hotel. Raindrops fell and burst over his forehead and shoulders. “One more time, baby,” he whispered. “Where are you?”

“Blake?” West asked.

Blake’s gaze darted over the hills. “I heard her scream.” *Come on*, he willed her to yell again, to give him some indication of which direction to go. She could be anywhere. He didn’t know how long she’d been gone or how much of a head start she had. He needed another scream.

“Do you still hear it?” West asked. “Did she yell again?”

The wail of an ambulance mucked up the silence.

“Damn it! She’s somewhere in the hills behind the hotel, but the ambulance is coming. Now, I can’t hear anything.” He waved an arm to draw the EMTs in his direction. Maybe when the deputy had his wits back, he could tell Blake which way Marissa went.

“Behind the hotel?” West made the sound of a falling missile. “That can’t be right. You must be getting the tail end of an echo from somewhere else. Those hills are mostly rock cliffs and—”

"Caves." Blake cut him off. "You're a genius, West." He shoved the phone into his pocket and ran straight for the trees.

Chapter Sixteen

The terrain behind the hotel was unexpectedly steep, slowing Blake within minutes. Thick craggy plants caught on his pant legs and tangled between his feet as he powered through the forest. Tiny mudslides seemed to sprout before his eyes, cutting slick paths between endless rocky snares. There were no trails. No well-trodden paths left by hikers or narrow byways formed by wildlife. There was only one obstacle after another, challenging his ability to stay upright and vigilant in the freezing rain.

He clipped his toe on the exposed roots of another towering tree and ground his teeth in frustration. This was nothing like the places he'd grown up hunting. Only black bears and bobcats would find this hellacious environment worth the trouble, and he had no interest in running into either.

Blake's phone vibrated in his pocket, and he pulled it free. "Garrett." He spoke in a hushed tone, eyes set to scan for any signs of Nash or Marissa.

"This is West. What do you have up there?"

Besides a broken toe and a growing ulcer, Blake

didn't have much. "I think I'm going the wrong way. She hasn't called out again. Not since the ambulance finally shut up. I've got nothing." He wiped rain from his eyes and peered up the mountain. The clouds had darkened the day, and thanks to the recent time change, they'd be out of daylight in under two hours.

Where was the path Marissa had taken up here? He scanned the area more closely, begging an overlooked set of footprints to appear. *There should be a path.* A lump filled his throat as the memory of her scream replayed in his mind. What if the last scream he'd heard was the last she'd ever make? What if he'd been too slow? Struggling up the wrong part of the mountain, wasting time while Nash ended her life? Blake forced the thoughts aside and refocused on two things he knew were fact: Marissa's scream had come from this general direction, and he needed a better plan. "You know anything about the caves up here?" he asked West. "Marissa said she did some spelunking up here. She said the caves were naturally camouflaged, but I don't see anything that looks like a cave."

"I've been around the other side of the mountain, skiing, but I don't know anything about the caves."

Blake marched ahead, boots sliding in the soft earth. "If Nash doesn't have her, I think she'll hole up in one of the caves until we get there."

"I'll get a team together." West's words were followed by utter silence.

Blake examined the phone's screen. "I'm almost out of bars."

"...on our way."

He sure as hell hoped so. At the pace he was moving, he'd be lucky to find one cave before nightfall, let alone explore multiple ones in search of his girl.

The sharp peal of a woman's scream tore through the air. An avalanche of leaves and branches blew into view along the eastern horizon where the sun had already dipped behind the mountain.

Blake moved doggedly eastward, toward the place where the leaves had rushed like a scarlet waterfall. Marissa's scream echoed in his heart and head. Why hadn't she made another sound? Was she unconscious? Was she dead? Did she fall or was she pushed? Rocks pressed against the soles of his boots, forcing gruesome images of Marissa into his mind. If she'd fallen as far as those leaves had tumbled, only to land on a pile of stones...

He forced himself to stop when the mound of earth and leaves came into view. Blake watched the perimeter for movement before inching forward to seek the pile's core.

Empty.

The setting sun cast shades of red and gold through the storm clouds giving the world a suddenly sinister appearance. He was thankful not to believe in omens. A small line in the earth caught his eye and he followed it steadily toward a rocky cliff ahead. The mark was consistent and deliberate, like someone dragging a broken limb or foot. He stepped cautiously over the leaf-covered ground, careful not to lose the trail or step headlong into Nash's trap.

Several feet farther, the mark stopped abruptly before a large oval stone. A thin sheet of moss drew him closer. Marissa had specifically mentioned the moss. *The moss is gorgeous near the caves' mouths.*

Blake moved stealthily toward the rock, senses peeled and muscles tensed to spring. The cave's mouth came into view seconds later, darkened by shadow and nearly invisible in the hillside. A mass of fallen rocks guarded the way.

He turned his back to the hill and eased forward, listening for footfalls, ragged breaths or any other sign that this was a trap. The hairs on the back of his neck stretched to attention as a long willowy shadow moved over the ground.

A feral grunt erupted, and Blake dropped back on instinct. Clay-scented wind rushed over his face. A thick, gnarled limb cut the air with a whoosh, missing his head by an inch.

He pressed off the ground in a flash, lunging for the shadow with his arms wide. His shoulder connected with the soft and narrow center of his attacker.

Marissa squeaked as air pushed from her core, and Blake's arms wound around her on instinct to cushion their collision with a cave wall. A massive branch clattered at their feet.

Joy filled his chest and lightened his heart. She wasn't dead, and Nash didn't have her. He cradled her to him as fat tears fell over her red cheeks. She sobbed into his shirt, and the moment of happiness was quickly replaced with fear. Her skin was like ice, covered in gooseflesh and red from the beating rain. "You're freezing." He stepped back and unzipped his jacket.

She teetered against the wall, balanced precariously on one foot.

"You're hurt." He squatted for a better look at her right leg. Blood had soaked through the material of her pants, down to her sock and into the top of her shoe.

Marissa gripped his shoulders and pulled him upright. "It's fine." Her teeth chattered. "Nothing's broken. My ankle is twisted. I can't put weight on it, and my shin is banged up from the fall. Something cut into my leg when I landed in the pile. My right calf is scratched pretty bad, but I'll live." She looked into his eyes with the saddest smile he'd ever seen. Another attempt to be strong and compartmentalize the horrors, he guessed. "Let's get out of here."

Blake helped her into his wet jacket and hugged her tight, willing his warmth over her. "It's not much, but it's dryer than you."

She zipped the offering up to her neck with trembling fingers. The chattering of her teeth increased, and her lips seemed to grow whiter. "I saw the fires on the news. Nash did that."

"I know." Blake rubbed his palms over her thin arms, hoping to create some heat from friction. "Smart girl."

"No," she sniffled. "No. I opened the door to invite the deputy inside, but Nash was already there. He forced his way inside. I fought back, but I had nowhere to go."

"It's okay. You got away again. That's all that matters." And getting her off this mountain. Blake assessed the cave for bats and bears. He couldn't see either, but he didn't want to stick around and press his luck. Marissa needed medical attention. "Is Nash hurt? Was he with you when you fell?"

"Yes, but I don't know if he was hurt." Marissa curled in on herself, measuring her breaths and breathing puffs of steam into the frigid air. "He's got a hunting jacket on. It's baggy and falls past his hips. I couldn't see any wounds. He might've been a little slower today." The inflection in her voice indicated further that she really wasn't sure. She was traumatized. Frightened and bleeding. "But he's mad," she whispered, "really mad."

"Okay." Time to go. "Help's on the way. We just need to hold down the fort." A small smile formed on his mouth. "I told West you'd be hiding in a cave." This woman was so much more than he could ask for. He needed to get her home safely so he could tell her exactly how true that was.

She wobbled for balance on her good leg. "I was in the larger cave about fifty yards up but I blew it," Marissa said. "I heard West's voice coming from a radio, and I thought you were right outside. I ran straight into Nash."

Blake hugged her closer. "He took the deputy's radio."

Marissa nodded.

"That's when I fell over the hill," she said. "He got a hold on me, and I did everything I could to shake him loose. He tried to hang on, but I went over the mountain. I figured the fall was the lesser of two evils, so I took my chances with the hill."

"I saw you fall," Blake said. "Where's Nash now?"

"I haven't seen him again."

Blake struggled for the right plan of action. West was scrambling the troops, but thanks to the stolen walkie-talkie, Nash would know that. Unless West had somehow found time to instruct his men otherwise. Nash had had them all in a tailspin today. So, what was his grand plan?

Blake couldn't wait around to find out. He needed to get Marissa off the mountain. Now.

But how? She couldn't walk on a busted ankle, and he couldn't carry her and keep her safe. His reflexes would be staunched, and his attention divided. Not to mention, one swift shove could send them both down the mountain.

Marissa swayed in his arms.

"Hey." He pressed one palm to her icy cheek. "Marissa?"

Her knees buckled, and her head rolled back.

Panic beat through Blake's head. He lowered her to the ground and checked her vitals. What was happening? Another head injury? Something internal? Her tiny puffs of breath were barely visible in the dank cave. The rise and fall of her chest was small and shallow. He checked her pulse and prayed. The tiny thrum barely registered against the pad of his fingers, but it was there.

There was also a new pool of blood by her foot.

Blake rolled the cuff of her pants for a look at the wound on Marissa's leg. The cuts were bad, much worse than she'd let on, and the blood flow hadn't stopped.

He shredded the hem of his shirt and wrapped her calf below the knee to encourage a clot. "Stay with me," he told her.

Where was his team? Where was West?

The snapping of twigs brought his scattered thoughts into focus. He tied the bandage and moved Marissa more deeply into the shadows, before slipping through the cave's mouth once more.

Another snap pulled Blake westward. Senses on alert and gun drawn, he moved silently through the burgeoning storm. Icy drops pelted his bare arms and stung his skin as he followed the sounds upward. Every moment Marissa suffered was another knife to his chest.

He circled the cave, climbing carefully higher for the broadest view of his surroundings. A team of agents came into sight below, roughly halfway between Marissa's cave and the hotel, and all were headed in the wrong direction.

He hurried back to the cave's entrance, using the limbs of reaching trees to keep himself upright. Once Marissa was safe, he could hunt Nash until they both died of old age if he had to. Right now, he needed to get her to those men. "I see the team," he announced, unsure if she'd woken in his absence. He scooped a baseball-sized stone from the cave floor, ready to throw it at the rescue squad marching away from him.

"No." Marissa's sweet voice warbled in fear.

He dropped the stone on instinct. Marissa was awake and frightened. The sudden realization that they weren't alone sent his right hand to his sidearm, flicking away the safety strap and blinking for focus in the dim cave light.

"Ah, ah, ah," the familiar voice taunted.

"Nash." Blake ground the word through clenched teeth.

The woman he loved moved slowly out of the shadows. A drip of her blood flowed over the hunting knife Nash had pressed securely to her jaw.

Chapter Seventeen

Marissa's heart hammered painfully, her breaths too short and swift to straighten her muddled thoughts. Her body ached and her teeth chattered, but the confusion was worst of all. She'd closed her eyes in comfort, tucked lovingly into Blake's arms, and a moment later, she'd awoken in the rough hands of a serial killer.

He'd yanked her carelessly upright, forcing a scream of pain from her lips. "Hello, darling," he'd snarled. "It's not nice of you to keep running away. You must know how hard I've worked for this reunion of ours. Setting fires. Distracting lawmen. Anything for you."

Marissa struggled to make sense of the change. Blake had been there, hadn't he? If he had, then where was he now? A new flash of panic coursed through her aching limbs. Her gaze dropped to the cave floor in search of him. Had Nash hurt Blake, or worse? "Where's Blake?" she cried. "What did you do to him?"

Nash gripped her harder, forcing her back against

his chest like he had twice before. "Stop talking about him!" Unlike their previous encounters, Nash only needed his left arm to still her this time. Marissa was weak and hurt, and he knew it. He'd seen her fall, watched her crash, struggle upright and hobble away. The distance between them had bought her time, but not enough. She'd stopped running, and he'd found her. Again.

"Aren't you going to thank me?" he whispered hotly against her cheek. "For giving your baby sister a ride home last night? It's dangerous to walk alone these days, you know."

"Thank you." The nonsensical words arrived with deep sincerity. Despite everything Nash had done, Marissa was thankful he hadn't hurt Kara. That he'd chosen her instead of her little sister for his wicked game.

Nash petted her soggy hair, then wrapped ice cold fingers over her forehead, smashing her tighter to his chest. "First I had to siphon the gas from her car," he complained, "but in the end everything worked out as I'd planned. Things usually do."

Lightning flashed outside the cave, illuminating her world and glinting brightly off the stainless-steel blade of a four-inch hunting knife in Nash's right hand.

"We're going to be together now." He rested his chin against the top of her head. The scruff of his unshaven face caught in her tangled hair with each wag of his jaw. The stink of cigarettes filled her senses, reminding her of his other attempts to kill her. "You're mine. Not his. However, he and I have a game going, so I'm going to need you to do something for me." He raised the knife to her throat and used it to push wads of leaf-encrusted hair away from her neck and shoulder. He angled his mouth near the bare, frozen skin of her jaw. "Call for him," he whispered. His hot, rancid breath sent a flood of vomit into her mouth.

Marissa recoiled, squirming uselessly for fresh air and freedom. "No."

Nash lifted the silver hunting blade to eye level. He twisted it inches away from her nose. "Call for him, or I'll cut you." His tongue darted out and licked the length of her jaw.

Her muscles knotted in disgust. She pressed her lips together and jerked her chin away. "No."

"Do it!" he growled. He released her head in favor of knotting calloused fingers in her hair. He shook until she lost her balance. "Don't be stupid." He pushed the tip of his blade into the soft flesh of her jaw. "You don't need to die for him. You die for me."

"Let her go, Nash." Blake's voice echoed through the cave. His hazy silhouette nearly filled the jagged opening. Rain sheeted behind him, forming puddles on the rocky floor.

Marissa's heart sputtered in a tide of mixed emotions. Blake had come to save her, but Nash only planned to let him watch her die.

Nash yanked upright, returning Marissa to her previous position, mashed against his chest by the pressure of one forearm. "There you are. The knight in shining armor. Come to steal my wife."

Blake moved slowly in their direction, eyes pinned on Nash and the knife. "She's not your wife. I've already taken all of those."

Marissa struggled for air as Nash clutched her tighter. She pried uselessly at his arm with weak and frozen fingers. She didn't want to die in a cave.

Blake raised his gun and pointed it over her head, presumably at Nash's. "You don't have to die today," he said in a tone that seemed to disagree, "but if you hurt her again, I promise you won't leave this cave without a body bag."

Nash laughed. He stepped back, opposing Blake's advance and dragging Marissa with him. His grip loosened slightly, and Marissa sucked air, clinging to his arm now, for balance on her good foot. "Won't it be poetic for Miss Lane and I to die together? One final romantic gesture. A grand finale, if you will." He floated the knife near her throat. "Here's what I have in mind. I kill her, then you kill me, and then later you kill yourself because how could you live with that?" He exaggerated each word of the sick proposal. "It's the perfect show of our commitment to one another, really."

Marissa whimpered. Hopefully Blake had a plan because she had nothing left, and the finale Nash had in mind was the stuff of her nightmares.

Nash danced the knife closer to her face.

Blake's steady cop expression didn't waver. Nash's words had bounced uselessly off him.

"You don't mind?" Nash taunted. "No skin off your nose?" He tapped the tip of Marissa's nose with the blade for emphasis before lowering the blade to beneath her jaw, He slid it carefully along the length of her throat, and she flinched when the steel nicked her collarbone, just above the zipper of her borrowed jacket. "Oops," he said carelessly, no doubt enjoying the madness racing over Blake's face. "Still think you have the upper hand?" Nash asked, gloating over the response he'd driven from Blake. He dragged the blade's tip into the groove between Marissa's breasts, then stopped it above her heart.

Blake swung his hands up, palms forward. "Stop. Don't hurt her." He released his offensive stance and allowed the gun to hang from the crook of one thumb. His Adam's apple bobbed, and his gaze slid from Nash's eyes to Marissa's for the first time. "What do you want, Nash?"

"What do I want?" he parroted in a mocking whine. "Don't you recognize a cry for help when you see one? I want to finish our game."

"What game?" Venom and hatred coated Blake's words.

Nash rubbed his cheek against Marissa's. "Has he told you our story?"

She shook her head quickly. Tears formed in her eyes, and her shoulders crept nearer her ears, attempting to put space between herself and the madman.

"Why don't you tell it?" Nash asked Blake.

"Why don't you let her go and we can finish this alone."

Nash made a show of twisting the knife against her breastbone. "First, put your gun down."

Blake lowered his weapon to the cave floor and released it, then straightened slowly, palms in plain sight. "Your turn. Let her go."

Marissa's eyelids fell shut. Blake had given in to Nash's demand, and nothing good could come from that.

Nash lifted the knife from Marissa's heart, and her head went light with relief. "First," he said, "tell the story. I like our story."

BLAKE'S MIND QUAKED with five years of awful memories. Their story, as Nash called it, was Blake's personal hell. He could recite the lengthy list of leads he'd followed to their inevitable dead ends in detail, but what good would that do? He locked his jaw, refusing to entertain Nash or his whims any longer.

Blake had plenty of old failures engraved on his heart, but he wouldn't add losing Marissa to them. He kept his chest carefully squared with Nash, concealing the spare firearm nestled in his waistband at the middle of his back. That gun was his last chance at fulfilling his promises. He'd vowed to keep Marissa safe, whatever the cost, and he would proudly fit Nash for a shiny new body bag.

"What are you waiting for?" Nash shifted Marissa in his grip, repositioning the knife at her side, just below her rib cage. "I'll get you started." He cleared his throat. "It's a tragic story of loves lost. Every time I find my perfect mate, she dies. First my mom, then my fiancée, then all the rest."

Blake forced himself not to lunge for the knife. It was a calculated risk he'd gladly take if it was only him who could get hurt. "You stalk innocent women. You attack them. Murder them. Which part of that sounds like love to you?"

"I marry them," Nash barked. "I give them the perfect gown, and the perfect ending. Then, I preserve them in the perfect moment. Forever." He ground his teeth and made a feral sound. "I created a legacy, and you ruined it!" A line of spittle landed on Marissa's soft cheek.

Blake winced. His stomach churned. Marissa was paler than before. She barely moved. The fight was gone from her, and that was scarier than anything Nash could say. Blake needed to speed this up and get her off this mountain. "The first one you took to the chapel was your fiancée."

"That's what I said."

Blake shook his head. The obvious finally clicked into place. "She's the one I didn't recognize." Nash hadn't begun killing immediately after her death, he'd taken her body to the chapel for her preservation in his "perfect moment." When that didn't satisfy him, he did it again, and again. "How did you do it? Steal her from the funeral home?"

"I made a donation to the grave digger's college fund."

Marissa's small mouth bowed down.

Blake inched closer, keeping the distraction going. Enticing Nash to stay focused on him instead of his captive. “Why are you doing this now? You’d stopped for so long.”

Nash heaved an angry sigh. “First, you promised to kill me. Then, you chased me for five years. *Five. Years*. I couldn’t stop moving. Couldn’t settle in or make a place for myself anywhere, then one day you just quit. You moved on. What did you think would happen when you did that? Did you think I’d get a new hobby? Collect trains? Build ships in bottles?”

So, it was Blake’s fault that Nash was at it again. He’d had a hand in the jogger’s murder and Marissa’s continued agony. His heart ached at the helplessness. At his utter inability to go back and change anything. He couldn’t make those things right. But he could end this. “If this is between us, then let her go.”

Nash shook his head. “No. You gave me time, and I got to know her. We fell in love.” He spread his fingers wider across Marissa’s ribs, skimming the pad of his thumb over her breast until Blake longed to break the digit off. “I knew the first moment I saw her that she had been worth waiting for,” Nash said. “I got a little overzealous and took a subpar substitute last month when this one changed her routine.” He made a droll face. “Plus, I was a little rusty, but again, that was your fault. Not mine.”

Blake’s fingers twitched with the need to pull his hidden weapon and fire. “You’re not getting out of this alive, Nash. Backup is on the way. It’s only a matter of time.”

"I don't expect to get out alive," he said flatly. Nash lowered the knife and used dirty fingers to part his jacket at the zipper, freeing the material from between his body and Marissa's. A blood-soaked patch clung to his side. Nash raised his eyebrows.

"Looks like someone shot you," Blake deadpanned. "You should probably get that looked at."

"It's infected. That's a point for you. I can't go to a hospital. You've put my face and my truck all over the news. More points for you. You got ahead of me this time, but the game's not over." His brows furrowed and his mouth bent down in contempt. "I *am* taking this one before I go. I see how you look at her. I've seen you touch her. I know you want her, but she's mine."

Blake's gaze slid to Marissa. He hadn't had a chance to tell her how he truly felt about her. That he'd fallen in love with her. That he needed her in his life because she made him want to be a better man, a better agent, and generally *more* than he thought was possible without her. If he screwed up again, he'd never get that chance.

Marissa's fierce expression set him off balance. Where he'd expected to find fear and agony, there was resolute determination. She narrowed her eyes on Blake and lifted one finger from Nash's arm, where she clung for balance.

Blake flicked his gaze to the seething killer, and Nash repositioned the blade against her ribs, ready to cut.

"Say goodbye," Nash demanded.

Marissa lifted a second finger from his arm and began to suck and puff air in a wild show of panic.

Nash turned his attention to her as she lifted a third finger from his arm and buckled her knees. He struggled to catch her weight with both hands, but she was limp and falling. A beautiful, brilliant dead weight that had completely broken Nash's concentration.

A deafening roar blasted through the cave as Blake's finger connected with the trigger of his hidden gun. Nash's head thrusted back, and the walls of the cave rattled. Nash landed on Marissa in a shower of rock and debris from above.

Blake dove to her side, tossing rubble and throwing Nash's body away from hers. He kicked the hunting blade through the cave's open door, and hoisted Marissa into his arms. "I've got you."

She tied her hands around his neck and pressed her lips to his cheek. "You did it," she whispered before resting her head against his swelling chest. "I knew you would."

A barrage of frantic voices beat against the wind, echoing and reverberating in the hills. The gunshot had surely drawn his team's attention. Blake strode carefully through the cave door and into the rain. His men and a mass of deputies jogged along a plateau several yards up. "Agent Garrett," someone called. "We heard gunfire."

"We need a medic," Blake called back. He adjusted Marissa in his grip. "She needs stitches and an IV. Warm blankets. There's a possible broken ankle, multiple lacerations. Extensive bruising and probably head trauma." Her legs dangled over the crook of his arm.

"Was she shot?" West called, running full speed along the plateau above.

"No." Blake shook his head. "Nash is dead. He's in the cave."

Blake's men continued past him to handle the crime scene.

West stopped at his side. "Marissa." He tipped his goofy sheriff's hat and smiled. "You're hard to get rid of."

She lifted a palm for a weak high five. "Like a bad rash."

"She needs medical attention," Blake complained.

"Here!" Cole raced into view, sliding through wet leaves and mud. The familiar silver stripes of a medical backpack gleamed in the waning sun. "The ski park sent an ATV to the plateau." He pointed in the direction from which he'd come. "There's an ambulance waiting just beyond that slope." He reached for Marissa, but Blake stepped away.

His eyes blurred with powerful unshed emotion. "I've got her."

And he had no intention of letting her go.

Chapter Eighteen

Marissa peeled her heavy lids open and squinted against the bright fluorescent light. The scents of bleach and Band-Aids tickled her nose. "Blake," she croaked, her throat impossibly dry.

"She's awake." Her mother's worried face swam into view.

Her mother. Marissa's frantic heart slowed by a fraction. She was safe. Nash was dead.

Blake had saved her, but where was he now?

"Thank goodness." Marissa's mother stroked her hair and kissed her cheeks. "We were terrified. You lost so much blood."

Marissa forced a smile on her tired face as she struggled for a better look at her surroundings. The simple hospital room was standard white on white with soft green accents and thick light-filtering curtains. The local news played softly on an old tube television anchored in the far corner near the ceiling. Nash's picture was wedged in the bottom corner of the screen. It was a face she longed to never see again, but knew full well he'd visit her dreams every night for years. She lifted a hand to set upon her mother's and discovered an IV line taped to her skin.

Her father levered himself out of an uncomfortable-looking chair and joined Marissa's mother at her bedside. Deep lines raced over her father's forehead. "She's got more color."

"You lost so much blood," her mother repeated.

"And Blake?" Marissa asked. "Did he go home?" Surely, he wouldn't have left without saying goodbye.

"Knock knock." A woman in a white lab coat sashayed through the door with a clipboard and a smile. "Good morning, Miss Lane. I'm glad to see you're awake."

Marissa's parents moved to the foot of her bed, eyes locked on the physician.

"I'm Dr. Starcher," the woman said. "I've been looking after you since your arrival last night."

"Thank you." Marissa choked.

The doctor poured a plastic cup of water from a bedside pitcher and handed it to her. "You had us all a little worried. I'm not sure how much your parents have had time to tell you, but you fractured your ankle. You have a mild concussion and were treated for hypothermia, multiple lacerations, extensive bruising and were given quite a few stitches for the cut on your leg."

Marissa blinked long and slow as the list of ailments and injuries settled in. She sipped the water and waited for her clogged throat to open again.

"You're one tough cookie," the doctor continued, "but I'll bet you've heard that a time or two." She cast a warm smile at Marissa's anxious parents before turning her attention to the pages on her clipboard. "After speaking to the agent and local sheriff about the week you've had, I'd say it's a miracle you're in as good of shape as you are." She tucked the board under one arm and gazed at the machinery near Marissa's bed. "All things considered, I guess dating a federal agent comes in handy at times like these."

"Agent Garrett?" Marissa guessed. Finally, someone who might tell her where he went.

Sadly, she and Blake weren't dating, but after all that they'd been through, she wished they were so much more. He was passionate and kind. Confident and funny. Blake had kept her safe but given her the space to be strong on her own. He trusted her choices, but always had her back. And that kiss. She smiled at the rising memory.

Blake was the one who set her soul on fire.

The doctor tipped her head toward the door. "That man hasn't left since we moved you in here. He set up shop right outside and personally monitored every guest until dawn, my nurses included. I think he may have finally fallen asleep."

Marissa's gaze jumped to the large silhouette suddenly filling her doorway. An exhausted-looking Blake leaned one shoulder against the jamb. Thick purple crescents underlined each sharp blue eye. A mix of relief and regret played over his handsome features.

Her heart swelled with happiness. "No. He doesn't sleep." Marissa patted the bed beside her legs.

The doctor bobbed her head. "There he is. I guess you're right." She gave Marissa a wink. "Everything looks good here. We'll get you some crutches for your ankle and a prescription for the pain. The cast comes off in a few weeks, but I'll write up your release papers this afternoon. How does that sound?"

"Wonderful," her mother said. "She'll be staying with us. I've made up her old room."

Marissa would have that discussion with her mom later. At the moment, she was afraid to take her eyes off of Blake in case he might disappear.

Blake inched into the room and took position against the wall.

"That sounds lovely." The doctor waved her parents through the doorway. "Let's talk a little more about that outside." She pulled the door closed behind them.

Marissa's heart sprinted along in her chest. Blake had stayed. What did that mean?

She patted her bed again.

Regret won the fight over relief on Blake's features. "I shouldn't. I'm big, and that bed is small, and you're covered in bruises. I don't want to hurt you."

Her gaze fell to her bare arms, visible in the ugly hospital gown. A rainbow of shades from brown to gold splayed over her pale skin. "Get over here."

His cheek twitched, and he obeyed, slowly. Blake stopped at her bedside and drifted his gaze over her face, neck and arms. "I'm so sorry."

She grabbed his wrist and tugged him down to

her. "Sit with me." She wiggled to make room and winced at the sudden pain in her ankle.

"You fractured your ankle," he said. "And that little scratch you told me about needed thirty-two stitches."

She shook her head. She'd heard all that already. "When do you have to leave?" she asked, needing to get the worst part of her day over with. How long did she have to enjoy the fantasy of a life with Blake in it? How long until she had to say goodbye?

Blake lowered himself onto the edge of her bed with a frown. "What do you mean? I'm not going anywhere." He flicked his attention to the door. "Unless you want me to."

She grabbed his hand and tugged him closer. "The case is over. You don't live here." She shot him with her best no-nonsense look. "Seems like the government would notice if it lost an agent."

"Right." Blake rubbed a heavy palm against his face. "I'm the guy who always has to leave." He peeked remorse-filled eyes at her. "I'm sorry."

"No." Marissa tugged his hand away from his face. "I meant how long will you be here? You must have to get back. You have a life in Louisville."

The worry lines slowly faded from Blake's brow. He searched her face with eager, curious eyes. "I'd like to have a life here."

Heat ran over Marissa's face, towing a wide smile behind it. "Yeah?"

"Yeah. It'll take some time to get the details in order," he said sheepishly, "and I'd have to commute an hour to work, but I love Shadow Point. I've got roots here, friends, family..." he lifted Marissa's hand to his lips. "Maybe even a girl."

"A woman," she corrected. "Absolutely."

Blake leaned closer, a moan rumbling in his chest. "Please tell me you feel well enough for a kiss."

"I do." Marissa's smiling lips met his, and she found everything she'd hoped for waiting there.

CHRISTMAS EVE ARRIVED with a foot of snow. Her ankle had finally healed, but it would be spring before she dared climb another mountain or anything more dangerous than a flight of stairs.

She poised her camera against one cheek and captured another image of Kara on horseback outside their parents' home. Large picturesque flakes made a magical backdrop to the photo. The shot would make a perfect gift for Kara's upcoming birthday.

"Merry Christmas," a familiar tenor called from behind her, setting her heart to sprint.

Marissa spun in anticipation of the only thing she'd prayed for this Christmas. Her smile fell slightly before she managed to recover. "Hi, West. Mr. Garrett. Merry Christmas." She shook Blake's brother's and father's hands. "What are you doing here?"

Marissa had nearly forgotten how similar West's voice was to Blake's. She'd spent plenty of time with the Garrett family after being released from the hospital, but she hadn't seen any of them since Blake was reassigned to a new case three weeks ago.

Their whirlwind romance had come to a screeching halt, along with Blake's house hunt in Shadow Point and their nightly phone calls. Though, she never fell asleep without receiving at least one email or text message letting her know he loved her. The notes were nice, but she dearly missed Blake's voice and the feel of his arms around her. So much so, that she almost understood how the other women in his past must have felt. It was harder than she'd expected to say goodbye, and she worried about him every day until she got that little note to say he was safe.

Mr. Garrett raised a telltale gift bag meant for wine. "I brought you a little something." He lifted a palm. "Don't open it just yet."

Marissa accepted the gift with a smile. "Thank you. I'll try to contain myself." She laughed and hooked her arm in his. "Let's go inside. Mom's made enough food to feed the town."

West waved them on. "I'll wait for Kara."

Marissa cast a curious look at West as he headed in Kara's direction.

Mr. Garrett patted her arm, drawing her attention back to him. "You know I took your dad shooting the other day. Beat him like a drum."

"Uh-huh." She nodded. "That wasn't how I heard it."

"Because he lies."

Marissa laughed as they rounded the side of her parents' home. A new line of cars filled the driveway. "What on earth?"

"Looks like there was a reason for all the food," Mr. Garrett mused.

"I guess so." They climbed the wide front steps to a porch lined in greenery and twinkle lights. A trio of women from her mother's book club waited at the door with cookie trays. "Hello," Marissa greeted them. "I didn't know you were coming, but I'm so glad you're here."

"We can't stay long," one woman said.

The front door swung open, and her mother motioned everyone inside. "Marissa, really. Why didn't you let them in?"

Marissa raised her palms.

Mr. Garrett dropped her arm and headed for the kitchen. He took her bottle of wine with him.

"Help take coats," her mother instructed.

"Sure." Marissa marveled at the house full of family and friends. Christmas music and warm apple cider wafted through the air. Every bough on the family tree hung low with white lights and handcrafted ornaments. Proof that two tragically untalented crafters had grown up there. "Why didn't you tell me so many people were coming?"

"Why did you think I started cooking yesterday?" She gave her daughter an encouraging smile. "You've been sad lately. I know you miss him. And who doesn't like a party?"

"I'm not sad," Marissa said.

She didn't have to ask who her mother had meant by *him*. There was only one him who set fire to Marissa's world. "I'm happy. I swear it. But I do miss him."

"I know." Her mom took the coats from Marissa and nudged her toward the guests. "On second thought, I can do this. You watch the door and mingle."

Marissa opened the front door ten times in the next hour, hugging and welcoming cousins and neighbors she hadn't seen in far too long. If she couldn't be with Blake today, this was definitely the next best thing.

The bell rang again, and she spun toward it with the same puff of anticipation that came with each knock. Though Blake had told her he couldn't make it for Christmas, she couldn't resist the hope he'd be the next person through the door.

Cole and his mother stood outside.

"Come in." She kissed their cheeks and pulled them inside. "Merry Christmas."

She couldn't stop herself from stealing a peek beyond them at Cole's empty car. Unfortunately, there were no federal agents waiting to surprise her on Christmas. A twinge of sadness tugged her heart.

She took their coats and offered them a drink, then went to collapse on the couch.

"Marissa?" Kara called from the porch. She knocked on the window and pressed her nose to the glass, mittens cupped around her face to peer inside.

Marissa laughed. "What are you doing?" She headed for the door shaking her head. Kara had done the same thing all her life, mostly when she was in trouble and needed Marissa's help to sneak past their parents. Considering Kara was now twenty-one and resided under her own roof, Marissa couldn't imagine what Kara was up to. "Goof." She opened the front door and stumbled back one big step.

Blake stood at the threshold, a small blue box in his hand. "Merry Christmas." He looked taller and broader and more handsome than she remembered. Three weeks had been far too long. His brown leather coat and jeans were speckled with melting snow, and the smile on his lips just begged for a kiss.

Kara bobbed into view. "Should we sneak him upstairs like the other boys? For old times' sake?"

Blake shot Kara a look. "I'm going to need a list of those boys' names."

"Me, too," Mr. Lane called from behind Marissa.

She twisted to find the crowded home had fallen silent. All eyes were on her and the man before her. She turned back in a flash, grabbing Blake's hands and towing him out of the cold. "I can't believe you're here."

"It's Christmas. Where else would I be?" Blake watched her silently with an expression she couldn't name.

Kara and West followed him inside and closed the door.

Marissa couldn't fight the smile on her lips. "You said you couldn't make it home for Christmas."

Blake's cheeks darkened. "I can't. Technically. I have to be somewhere first thing in the morning."

"You came all the way back for one night?" Marissa blushed at the thoughts of what they could accomplish in those precious few hours, and she wished more than ever that the nosy crowd would go back to minding its own business instead of hanging on her every word. "You didn't have to do that." It was just too much. "You don't need to zigzag the country to keep me happy." She'd known exactly what she was getting into when she'd fallen in love with Federal Agent Blake Garrett.

"I know. I'm here because I couldn't stay away." He took her left hand in his right. "I had to fly home tonight because I couldn't go another day without asking you something."

A hush rolled through the room as Blake lowered onto his knee and lifted the tiny blue box in Marissa's direction.

She startled. "Yes." Was this a proposal? "Yes."

"Wait." Blake chuckled. "I'm not finished."

"Hurry." Her eyes filled with tears and she covered her mouth to laugh.

The room giggled softly beside her.

Blake pinned her with glossy blue eyes. "I know this probably seems soon, and I haven't been around as much as I'd like to," he began. "I wish I could tell you that second part will change, but I can't. What I can tell you is that I've never loved or admired anyone the way I do you. You astound and impress me every day with your strength, your bravery and your heart for this world and everything in it. I can't promise to be here as much as other husbands, but if you'll let me, I will vow to love, honor and protect you every day of your life. I'll rock climb, parasail, scuba dive, or any other crazy thing you want. As long as I can do it with you."

Marissa's heart caught on that blessed word, *husband*. Blake Garrett wanted her to be his wife. She lowered to her knees and wrapped her arms around the man she loved more than all the things on Earth combined.

"Marry me?" he asked.

She pulled back enough to press her lips to his and was instantly folded into his arms. He deepened the kiss and she doubled his efforts.

Kara cleared her throat obnoxiously. "Excuse me."

A round of giggles pulled Marissa from another perfect kiss. The only sort Blake seemed to deliver.

He pressed his forehead to hers, creating a private space for them.

"We're waiting for an answer," someone called. "We came for the answer."

Marissa's jaw dropped, and the massive impromptu party suddenly made much more sense. "You planned this?"

"Yeah." Blake's forehead rocked against hers. "How'd I do?"

"Amazing," she whispered.

"Marry me?" he asked again, snaking his arms tighter around her waist and dragging her impossibly closer. "Don't make me beg in front of all these people."

"Yes." She nodded and smiled, then moved her mouth to his ear. "I will never resent you for your absence in my days or your dedication to this job. I love that you want to save the world, and I can't wait to explore it at your side."

"Yes?" Blake asked.

"Yes," she repeated. "Yes, to all of it. Except scuba diving. No more of that. Ever."

Somewhere nearby, a champagne cork popped, and Blake's dad cheered.

The crowd broke into applause as Blake lifted a fist in victory and kissed her once more. Exactly as he would for as long as they both should live.

* * * * *

Look for the next book in Julie Anne Lindsey's PROTECTORS OF CADE COUNTY *miniseries, THE SHERIFF'S SECRET, available next month!*

SPECIAL EXCERPT FROM

Tucker Cahill returns to Gilt Edge, Montana, with no choice but to face down his haunted past when a woman's skeletal remains are found near his family's ranch—but he couldn't have prepared for a young woman seeking vengeance and finding much more.

Read on for a sneak preview of
HERO'S RETURN,
A CAHILL RANCH NOVEL
from New York Times bestselling author
B.J. Daniels!

Skeletal Remains Found in Creek

The skeletal remains of a woman believed to be in her late teens or early twenties were discovered in Miner's Creek outside of Gilt Edge, Montana, yesterday. Local coroner Sonny Bates estimated that the remains had been in the creek for somewhere around twenty years.

Sheriff Flint Cahill is looking into missing-persons cases from that time in the hopes of identifying the victim. If anyone has any information, they are encouraged to call the Gilt Edge Sheriff's Department.

"No, Mrs. Kern, I can assure you that the bones that were found in the creek are not those of your nephew Billy," Sheriff Flint Cahill said into the phone at his desk. "I saw Billy last week at the casino. He was alive and well… No, it takes longer than a week for a body to decompose to nothing but bones. Also, the skeletal remains that were found were a young woman's… Yes, Coroner Sonny Bates can tell the difference."

He looked up as the door opened and his sister, Lillie, stepped into his office. From the scowl on her face, he didn't have to ask what kind of mood she was in. He'd been expecting her, given that he had their father locked up in one of the cells.

"Mrs. Kern, I have to go. I'm sorry Billy hasn't called you, but I'm sure he's fine." He hung up with a sigh. "Dad's in the back sleeping it off. Before he passed out, he mumbled about getting back to the mountains."

A very pregnant Lillie nodded but said nothing. Pregnancy had made his sister even prettier. Her long dark hair framed a face that could only be called adorable. This morning, though, he saw something in her gray eyes that worried him.

He waited for her to tie into him, knowing how she felt about him arresting their father for being drunk and disorderly. This wasn't their first rodeo. And like always, it was Lillie who came to bail Ely out—not his bachelor brothers Hawk and Cyrus, who wanted to avoid one of Flint's lectures.

He'd been telling his siblings that they needed to do something about their father. But no one wanted to face the day when their aging dad couldn't continue to spend most of his life in the mountains gold panning and trapping—let alone get a snoot full of booze every time he finally hit town again.

"I'll go get him," Flint said, lumbering to his feet. Since he'd gotten the call about the bones being found at the creek, he hadn't had but a few hours' sleep. All morning, the phone had been ringing off the hook. Not with leads on the identity of the skeletal remains—just residents either being nosy or worried there was a killer on the loose.

"Before you get Dad…" Lillie seemed to hesitate, which wasn't like her. She normally spoke her mind without any encouragement at all.

He braced himself.

"A package came for Tuck."

That was the last thing Flint had expected out of her mouth. "To the saloon?"

"To the ranch. No return address."

Flint felt his heart begin to pound harder. It was the first news of their older brother Tucker since he'd left home right after high school. Being the second oldest, Flint had been closer to Tucker than with his younger brothers. For years, he'd feared him dead. When Tuck had left like that, Flint had suspected his brother was in some kind of trouble. He'd been sure of it. But had it been something bad enough that Tucker hadn't felt he could come to Flint for help?

"Did you open the package?" he asked.

Lillie shook her head. "Hawk and Cyrus thought about it but then called me."

He tried to hide his irritation that one of them had called their sister instead of him, the darned sheriff. His brothers had taken over the family ranch and were the only ones still living on the property, so it wasn't a surprise that they would have received the package. Which meant that whoever had sent it either didn't know that Tucker no longer lived there or they thought he was coming back for some reason.

Because Tucker was on his way home? Maybe he'd sent the package and there was nothing to worry about.

Unfortunately, a package after all this time didn't necessarily bode well. At least not to Flint, who came by his suspicious nature naturally as a lawman. He feared it might be Tucker's last effects.

"I hope *you* didn't open it."

Lillie shook her head. "You think this means he's coming home?" She sounded so hopeful it made his heart ache. He and Tucker had been close in more ways than age. Or at least he'd thought so. But something had been going on with his brother his senior year in high school and Flint had no idea what it was. Or if trouble was still dogging his brother.

For months after Tucker left, Flint had waited for him to return. He'd been so sure that whatever the trouble was, it was temporary. But after all these years, he'd given up any hope. He'd feared he would never see his brother again.

"Tell them not to open it. I'll stop by the ranch and check it out."

Lillie met his gaze. "It's out in my SUV. I brought it with me."

Flint swore under his breath. What if it had a bomb in it? He knew that was overly dramatic, but still, knowing his sister… There wasn't a birthday or Christmas present that she hadn't shaken the life out of as she'd tried to figure out what was inside it. "Is your truck open?" She nodded. "Wait here."

He stepped out into the bright spring day. Gilt Edge sat in a saddle surrounded by four mountain ranges still tipped with snow. Picturesque, tourists came here to fish its blue-ribbon trout stream. But winters were long and a town of any size was a long way off.

Sitting in the middle of Montana, Gilt Edge also had something that most tourists didn't see. It was surrounded by underground missile silos. The one on the Cahill Ranch was renown because that was where their father swore he'd seen a UFO not only land, but also that he'd been forced on board back in 1967. Which had made their father the local crackpot.

Flint took a deep breath, telling himself to relax. His life was going well. He was married to the love of his life. But still, he felt a foreboding that he couldn't shake off. A package for Tucker after all these years?

The air this early in the morning was still cold, but there was a scent to it that promised spring wasn't that far off. He loved spring and summers here and had been looking forward to picnics, trail rides and finishing the yard around the house he and Maggie were building.

He realized that he'd been on edge since he'd gotten the call about the human bones found in the creek. Now he could admit it. He'd felt as if he was waiting for the other shoe to drop. And now this, he thought as he stepped to his sister's SUV.

The box sitting in the passenger-side seat looked

battered. He opened the door and hesitated for a moment before picking it up. For its size, a foot-and-half-size cube, the package was surprisingly light. As he lifted the box out, something shifted inside. The sound wasn't a rattle. It was more a rustle like dead leaves followed by a slight thump.

Like his sister had said, there was no return address. Tucker's name and the ranch address had been neatly printed in black—not in his brother's handwriting. The generic cardboard box was battered enough to suggest it had come from a great distance, but that wasn't necessarily true. It could have looked like that when the sender found it discarded and decided to use it to send the contents. He hesitated for a moment, feeling foolish. But he heard nothing ticking inside. Closing the SUV door, he carried the box inside and put it behind his desk.

"Aren't you going to open it?" Lilly asked, wide-eyed.

"No. You need to take Dad home." He started past his sister but vacillated. "I wouldn't say anything to him about this. We don't want to get his hopes up that Tucker might be headed home. Or make him worry."

She glanced at the box and nodded. "Did you ever understand why Tuck left?"

Flint shook his head. He was torn between anger and sadness when it came to his brother. Also fear. What had happened Tucker's senior year in high school? What if the answer was in that box?

"By the way," he said to his sister, "I didn't arrest Dad. Ely voluntarily turned himself in last night." He shrugged. Flint had never understood his father any more than he had his brother Tuck. To this day, Ely swore that he had been out by the missile silo buried in the middle of their ranch when a UFO landed, took him aboard and did experiments on him.

Then again, their father liked his whiskey and always had.

"You all right?" he asked his sister when she still said nothing.

Lillie nodded distractedly and placed both hands over the baby growing inside her. She was due any day now. He hoped the package for Tucker wasn't something that would hurt his family. He didn't want anything upsetting his sister in her condition. But he could see that just the arrival of the mysterious box had Lillie worried. She wasn't the only one.

TUCKER CAHILL SLOWED his pickup as he drove through Gilt Edge. He'd known it would be emotional, returning after all these years. He'd never doubted he would return—he just hadn't expected it to take nineteen years. All that time, he'd been waiting like a man on death row, knowing how it would eventually end.

Still, he was filled with a crush of emotion. *Home.* He hadn't realized how much he'd missed it, how much he'd missed his family, how much he'd missed his life in Montana. He'd been waiting for this day, dreading it and, at the same time, anxious to return at least once more.

As he started to pull into a parking place in

front of the sheriff's department, he saw a pregnant woman come out followed by an old man with long gray hair and a beard. His breath caught. Not sure if he was more shocked to see how his father had aged—or how pregnant and grown up his little sister, Lillie, was now.

He couldn't believe it as he watched Lillie awkwardly climb into an SUV, the old man going around to the passenger side. He felt his heart swell at the sight of them. Lillie had been nine when he'd left. But he could never forget a face that adorable. Was that really his father? He couldn't believe it. When had Ely Cahill become an old mountain man?

He wanted to call out to them but stopped himself. As much as he couldn't wait to see them, there was something he had to take care of first. Tears burned his eyes as he watched Lillie drive their father away. It appeared he was about to be an uncle. Over the years while he was hiding out, he'd made a point of following what news he could from Gilt Edge. He'd missed so much with his family.

He swallowed the lump in his throat as he opened his pickup door and stepped out. The good news was that his brother Flint was sheriff. That, he hoped, would make it easier to do what he had to do. But facing Flint after all this time away... He knew he owed his family an explanation, but Flint more than the rest. He and his brother had been so close—until his senior year.

He braced himself as he pulled open the door to the sheriff's department and stepped in. He'd let everyone down nineteen years ago, Flint especially. He doubted his brother would have forgotten—or forgiven him.

But that was the least of it, Flint would soon learn.

AFTER HIS SISTER LEFT, Flint moved the battered cardboard box to the corner of his desk. He'd just pulled out his pocketknife to cut through the tape when his intercom buzzed.

"There's a man here to see you," the dispatcher said. He could hear the hesitation in her voice. "He says he's your *brother*?" His family members never had the dispatcher announce them. They just came on back to his office. *"Your brother, Tucker?"*

Flint froze for a moment. Hands shaking, he laid down his pocketknife as relief surged through him. Tucker was alive and back in Gilt Edge? He had to clear his throat before he said, "Send him in."

He told himself he wasn't prepared for this and yet it was something he'd dreamed of all these years. He stepped around to the front of his desk, half-afraid of what to expect. A lot could have happened to his brother in nineteen years. The big question, though, was why come back now?

As a broad-shouldered cowboy filled his office doorway, Flint blinked. He'd been expecting the worst.

Instead, Tucker looked great. Still undeniably handsome with his thick dark hair and gray eyes like the rest of the Cahills, Tucker had filled out from the teenager who'd left home. Wherever he'd been, he'd apparently fared well. He appeared to have been doing a lot of physical labor, because he was buff and tanned.

Flint was overwhelmed by both love and regret as he looked at Tuck, and furious with him for making him worry all these years.

"Hello, Flint," Tucker said, his voice deeper than Flint remembered.

He couldn't speak for a moment, afraid of what would come out of his mouth. The last thing he wanted to do was drive his brother away again. He wanted to hug him and slug him at the same time.

Instead, he said, voice breaking, "Tuck. It's so damned good to see you," and closed the distance between them to pull his older brother into a bear hug.

TUCKER HUGGED FLINT, fighting tears. It had been so long. Too long. His heart broke at the thought of the lost years. But Flint looked good, taller than Tucker remembered, broader shouldered, too.

"When did you get so handsome?" Tucker said as he pulled back, his eyes still burning with tears. It surprised him that they were both about the same height. Like him, Flint had filled out. With their dark hair and gray eyes, they could almost pass for twins.

The sheriff laughed. "You know darned well that you're the prettiest of the bunch of us."

Tucker laughed, too, at the old joke. It felt good. Just like it felt good to be with family again. "Looks like you've done all right for yourself."

Flint sobered. "I thought I'd never see you again."

"Like Dad used to say, I'm like a bad penny. I'm bound to turn up. How is the old man? Was that him I saw leaving with Lillie?"

"You didn't talk to them?" Flint sounded both surprised and concerned.

"I wanted to see you first." Tucker smiled as Flint laid a hand on his shoulder and squeezed gently before letting go.

"You know how he was after Mom died. Now he spends almost all of his time up in the mountains panning gold and trapping. He had a heart attack a while back, but it hasn't slowed him down. There's no talking any sense into him."

"Never was." Tucker nodded as a silence fell between them. He and Flint had once been so close. Regret filled him as Flint studied him for a long moment before he stepped back and motioned him toward a chair in his office.

Closing the door, Flint settled into his chair behind his desk. Tucker dragged up one of the office chairs.

"I wondered if you wouldn't be turning up, since Lillie brought in a package addressed to you when she came to pick up Dad. He often spends a night in my jail when he's in town. Drunk and disorderly."

Tucker didn't react to that. He was looking at the battered brown box sitting on Flint's desk. *"A package?"* His voice broke. No one could have known he was coming back here unless…

Don't miss
HERO'S RETURN,
available March 2018 wherever
HQN Books and ebooks are sold.

www.Harlequin.com

The twisted machinations of a ruthless cult leader have robbed Lola Dayton of her life—and her baby. Now it's up to Sheriff Flint Cahill to find the truth buried beneath Lola's secrets and her family's lies.

Read on for a sneak preview of COWBOY'S REDEMPTION, part of **THE MONTANA CAHILLS** *series from* New York Times *bestselling author B.J. Daniels!*

"I had nowhere else to go." Her words came out in a rush. "I was so worried that you wouldn't be here." She burst into tears and slumped as if physically exhausted.

He caught her, swung her up into his arms and carried her into the house, kicking the door closed behind him. His mind raced as he tried to imagine what could have happened to bring her to his door in Gilt Edge, Montana, in the middle of the night and in this condition.

"Sit here," he said as he carried her in and set her down in a kitchen chair before going for the first-aid kit. When he returned, he was momentarily taken aback by the memory of this woman the first time he'd met her. She wasn't beautiful in the classic sense. But she was striking, from her wide violet eyes fringed with pale lashes to the silk of her long blond hair. She had looked like an angel, especially in the long white dress she'd been wearing that night.

That was over a year ago and he hadn't seen her since. Nor had he expected to since they'd met initially several hundred miles from the ranch. But whatever had struck him about her hadn't faded. There was something flawless about her—even as scraped up and bruised as she was. It made him furious at whoever was responsible for this.

"Can you tell me what happened?" he asked as he began to clean the cuts.

"I…I…" Her throat seemed to close on a sob.

"It's okay, don't try to talk." He felt her trembling and could see that she was fighting tears. "This cut under your eye is deep."

She said nothing, looking as if it was all she could do to keep her eyes open. He took in her torn and filthy dress. It was long, like the white one he'd first seen her in, but faded. It reminded him of something his grandmother might have worn to do housework in. She was also thinner than he remembered.

As he gently cleaned her wounds, he could see dark circles under her eyes, and her long braided hair was in disarray with bits of twigs and leaves stuck in it.

The night he'd met her, her plaited hair had been pinned up at the nape of her neck—until he'd released it, the blond silk dropping to the center of her back.

He finished his doctoring, put away the first-aid kit and wondered how far she'd come to find him and what she had been through to get here. When he returned to the kitchen, he found her standing at the back window, staring out. As she turned, he saw the fear in her eyes—and the exhaustion.

Colt desperately wanted to know what had happened to her and how she'd ended up on his doorstep. He hadn't even thought that she'd known his name. "Have you had anything to eat?"

"Not in the past forty-eight hours or so," she said, squinting at the clock on the wall as if not sure what day it was. "And not all that much before that."

He'd been meaning to get into Gilt Edge and buy some groceries. "Sit and I'll see what I can scare up," he said as he opened the refrigerator. Seeing only one egg left, he said, "How do you feel about pancakes? I have chokecherry syrup."

She nodded and attempted a smile. She looked skittish as a newborn calf. Worse, he sensed that she was having second thoughts about coming here.

She licked her cracked lips. "I have to tell you. I have to explain—"

"It's okay. You're safe here."